On *American Meteor*

"[Walt Whitman] hovers over [*American Meteor*], just as Mark Twain's spirit pervaded *The Boy in His Winter.* . . . Like all Mr. Lock's books, this is an ambitious work, where ideas crowd together on the page like desperate men on a battlefield."
—*Wall Street Journal*

On *The Port-Wine Stain*

"Lock's novel engages not merely with [Edgar Allan Poe and Thomas Dent Mütter] but with decadent fin de siècle art and modernist literature that raised philosophical and moral questions about the metaphysical relations among art, science and human consciousness. The reader is just as spellbound by Lock's story as [his novel's narrator] is by Poe's. . . . Echoes of Wilde's *The Picture of Dorian Gray* and Freud's theory of the uncanny abound in this mesmerizingly twisted, richly layered homage to a pioneer of American Gothic fiction." —*New York Times Book Review*

On *Feast Day of the Cannibals*

"Lock does not merely imitate 19th-century prose; he makes it his own, with verbal flourishes worthy of Melville." —*Gay & Lesbian Review*

On *American Follies*

"*Ragtime* in a fever dream. . . . When you mix 19th-century racists, feminists, misogynists, freaks, and a flim-flam man, the spectacle that results might bear resemblance to the contemporary United States." —*Library Journal* (starred review)

On *Tooth of the Covenant*

"Splendid. . . . Lock masters the interplay between nineteenth-century [Nathaniel] Hawthorne and his fictional surrogate, Isaac, as he travels through Puritan New England. The historical details are immersive and meticulous."
—*Foreword Reviews* (starred review)

VOICES
in the
DEAD HOUSE

VOICES
in the
DEAD HOUSE

Norman Lock

Bellevue Literary Press
New York

First published in the United States in 2022
by Bellevue Literary Press, New York

For information, contact:
Bellevue Literary Press
90 Broad Street
Suite 2100
New York, NY 10004
www.blpress.org

Library of Congress Cataloging-in-Publication Data
Names: Lock, Norman, author.
Title: Voices in the dead house / Norman Lock.
Description: First edition. | New York : Bellevue Literary Press, 2022.
| Series: American novels series
Identifiers: LCCN 2021033510 | ISBN 9781954276017 (paperback)
| ISBN 9781954276024 (epub)
Subjects: LCGFT: Historical fiction.
Classification: LCC PS3562.O218 V65 2022 | DDC 813/.54--dc23/
eng/20211012
LC record available at https://lccn.loc.gov/2021033510

Bellevue Literary Press would like to thank all its generous
donors—individuals and foundations—for their support.

 This project is supported in part by an award
from the National Endowment for the Arts.

This publication is made possible by the New York
State Council on the Arts with the support of the Office
of the Governor and the New York State Legislature.

Book design and composition by Mulberry Tree Press, Inc.

Bellevue Literary Press is committed to ecological stewardship in our
book production practices, working to reduce our impact on
the natural environment.

♻ This book is printed on acid-free paper.

Manufactured in the United States of America
First Edition

1   3   5   7   9   8   6   4   2

paperback ISBN: 978-1-954276-01-7
ebook ISBN: 978-1-954276-02-4

To Helen
On Our Fiftieth Wedding Anniversary

*As I list to the dirge, the voices of men and women
wreck'd.*

—Walt Whitman

*. . . and one lay stark and still with covered face, as
a comrade gave his name to be recorded before they
carried him away to the dead house.*

—Louisa May Alcott

VOICES
in the
DEAD HOUSE

WALT WHITMAN

Washington City
DECEMBER 21, 1862–JANUARY 21, 1863

*A*fter the news from Fredericksburg, I went in search of my brother George, whose name had been listed among the wounded in the *Tribune*. Dead or dying men lay everywhere, as well as what could scarcely be called men, having been reshaped by cannon and musket shot into what is more often seen in butchers' stalls. On perfect terms of equality, the victorious and the defeated—those no longer quick—were being translated into meat, while the maimed hankered to be done with their mortal part and to put behind them their shattered bones. The noise of armies having ebbed away, the stunned birds had found their songs and the river its voice, which sounded raw and chiding, as it was carried windward across Virginian fields whose winter harvest would be ample for what gnaws.

I sat on the ground and, like Shakespeare's Richard II, would have told myself sad stories of the death of kings, if not for the amputated arms and legs heaped beneath a tree. Astonishment will sometimes numb the grated nerve and staunch the flood of sharp sensations, as a jet of blood is by a cauterizing iron. I was too overcome for stories. I had believed myself to be inured to gore and stench, having dressed the awful wounds of streetcar drivers caught in the mangle of their trade, at the New York Hospital, near Broadway, where Anthony Trollope, famous for his *Barchester Towers*, once fainted dead away during a tour of the city's underworld. I was not inured. I could have roomed in a charnel house and still have been unmanned by the Battle of Fredericksburg's bloody aftermath—nearly thirteen thousand Union casualties, and not an acre of ground given by Lee's shabby graybacks.

Meanwhile, unconcerned by men's folly, the December sun shone on the blasted town, the harrowed fields, and the icy waters of the Rappahannock.

I found George in a field hospital across the river in Falmouth. He had a hole in his cheek from a bullet shot clean through it. Otherwise, he was fit and raring to have another go at Johnny Reb. I kept him company over Christmas—joyless and bleak—and on the twenty-eighth, I left him at Falmouth, where Ambrose Burnside's battered Union army would winter. Together with some of the most gravely wounded, I rode in an uncovered railway wagon to Aquia Landing, on the western bank of the broad

Potomac. From there, we traveled by government steamer forty-five miles upriver to Washington City and the Sixth Street wharf.

At Falmouth, in the Lacy mansion requisitioned by the Union army, I had watched Clara Barton comfort the stricken boys waiting for their smashed limbs to be added to the reeking pile. There I took it into my head to make myself useful at one or another of the impromptu hospitals that have sprung up like puffballs in the rain of blood that has been falling on our young men ever since the skedaddle at First Bull Run bruised the Union's vanity. The best of them, Armory Square Hospital, across the canal from the President's House, had been raised on the grounds of the old Columbia arsenal. Ventilated and efficiently arranged for the grim business conducted there, it took its inspiration from the British hospitals built during an earlier season of butchery, the Crimean War—"that house of misery," as Longfellow put it— where Florence Nightingale got her start.

Now by the gray sun's rays dispersed by rows of grimy panes, I watch Death work on the flesh of boys who were once beautiful to me. For in tranquil days, I knew and loved them—or those so very like them as to be their brothers, as they are mine. I was with them in the rough-and-tumble surf off Paumanok when the Atlantic turned incarnadine and, later, when the water and the sky blackened. At Coney Island, I consorted with robust youths who

had come over on the boats from Manhattan to fish,
dig for quahog and razor clams, and disport themselves—affectionate and manly—in Eddy and Hart's
hotel, beside Gravesend Bay. On Gowanus Creek's
willowed shore, I loafed with clerks and with butchers' boys still dressed in their killing clothes. And on
flying picnics to Greenport, I bathed in the Peconic,
invigorated by the company of soap-locked roughs
from the Bronx, as well as clean-limbed, industrious fellows employed by the custom house. I made
no distinction—I make none now. They are with me,
men of a generation, and ever so many generations
hence. They and I are atoms of the one great soul,
plebeians of the rude democracy of these States and
territories, which shall not end until the kosmos itself
ends in fiery dissolution.

I, too, have felt my shoulders ache after a day's
walk behind the plow, my face tanned by the sun or,
having labored in the foundry, by the Bessemer furnace. At night, returning home on the streetcar, my
ears have rung with the roar of the rotary presses—my
fingers black with news of calamity. (Joys were few
and far between amid the jostling items.) On tow-
paths and the decks of sailing ships, I've felt the haw-
ser bite my palms, and on the pavements, the weight
of a heavy sack jammed with oysters raked up from
the bay to sell to the barrooms of Brooklyn Heights
and Red Hook. I've stopped at cheap eateries to savor
their delicious flesh with my comrades. I have drunk

as heartily as they in East Side saloons before going to watch an Irishman and a German lay waste to each other with bare-knuckled aplomb. I enter high and low alike. I am not put off by the *demos* nor daunted by manifestations of great wealth. Nothing is beneath my dignity—no man, woman, or purpose, no venue or assembly where joy and freedom are entertained. Nor does the supercilious look of an Astor or a Vanderbilt abash me. I keep my hat on and push in.

Death, too, is democratic and makes no distinction.

Walt, you make too much of yourself! Instead of singing lauds to your imperturbability, descant upon the "nightingales" who do for the sick and wounded, drawing compassion by the bucketful from the well of kindness with bloody hands.

I MARVEL AT THE WOMEN who go about their business amid Death's grim warrants, bathing soiled or putrid bodies, changing dressings, anointing wounds with powders and unguents. They talk admiringly of the expert needlework of the surgeons, whose material is not cambric or even silk, but finer stuff. (Silk cannot blush or grow expectant in the presence of a beloved.) See how the woman lies across the man's body while the surgeon saws the devastated arm, or how lovingly she encircles a boy's narrow shoulders with her arms while the calm practitioner removes a minié ball from his thigh. They do not shirk in their appalling transactions with Death—these women who bestow chaste kisses on the lips of my camerados! I swear you are lovelier to me than the debutante waltzing with the heir to a fortune in ships or coal—lovelier even than the mother, her new babe in her arms, exhausted by her long accouchement. Wearing your soiled aprons, you are as radiant as mothers and outshine the glamour of debutantes!

The dark-haired nurse I saw at Union Hospital this morning didn't flinch when Death wrung from the boyish captain of artillery the last drop of life, although the delicate nostrils betrayed her loathing and gentility. She is new to the wards and will soon be unaffected by the contents of chamber pots and slop pails, if she sticks. I think she will. She did not have the look of someone who will turn and run. I've seen other well-meaning persons overcome by the grisly sights and foul odors. But that imposing young woman, her hands chapped by carbolic, she will stick. I saw the resolve in her black eyes. Twice she glanced at me, as if she knew me. Perhaps she had seen my likeness somewhere.

Walt, will you never tire of yourself? You're a humbug—truth be told—and the truth—the whole of it—can never be told in verse or prose, no matter how the book may shock by its gritty particulars. You remind me of a stage actor who, having raised his purple-togaed arm to salute the Roman mob, glances at his hand, and adjusts it. It's all an attitude, Whitman, a pose. *Leaves of Grass* is not the frank embrace of the world that you claim for it, but a pool into which Narcissus gazes, enraptured by his own beauty.

"Of the *world*?" When have you ever been modest? In *Leaves of Grass,* you would wind your arms around the kosmos, and you will not finish with it till you've annexed every nook and cranny of creation—I won't say "God's." I don't think he says *my* name. (I agree with Thomas Paine that He, who has a million worlds to oversee, would not have bothered to send His son to Earth and an earthly death to chastise Adam and Eve for the sake of one purloined apple.)

Thou P. T. Barnum of the Word, why are you here? Are there no good works to be done in Brooklyn? Does the East Side want for casualties? Everywhere wretchedness is at the flood. You can take your pick of a suffering humanity to cosset. You did what you had set out to do: You found your brother in a shebang after the Union army took a shellacking below Marye's Heights. Go home, Whitman! There's nothing for you here in Washington. If you enjoy the sight of swine in the streets (I mean those on the hoof, not the jackanapes in striped trousers who root in the troughs of patronage), you can return to Long Island and muck about in the farmers' sties. What does Manhattan lack that the capital possesses? You can see swindlers in yellow shoes there as easily as in the District of Columbia. The rats wear the same

silk hats on Wall Street as they do on Pennsylvania
Avenue. As for splendor, why I'd sooner see the sun
rise out of the sea off Orient Point than the glister
of sewage and dead cats floating in the Washington
City Canal!

"I swear I'm no humbug!" The asservation jumped
from my mouth.

"Bugger you!" says a young soldier, eyeing me
warily from where he lies on his cot.

"Sorry, I didn't mean to disturb you." I approach
the wounded man—he is hardly more than a boy. I
push the long brown hair aside. I touch the feverish
brow. "Your forehead's damp."

"My jism's backed up for lack of cunt. Any chance
you have one in your pantaloons?"

"That's the fever talking."

"I don't care a fuck!"

Walt, you are more than twoscore years. You've
been abroad in the world since you were twelve.
You've gone among press operators and surly editors,
who do not spare a young fellow's ears. You visited
maimed stage drivers at New York Hospital and
dressed the wounds of soldiers sent north to mend
after the bloody blunders committed by Generals
McClellan, Pope, and Burnside. Good Anglo-Saxon
words can't jar the troubadour of democracy.

The young man growls. "It's hotter in here than
Old Nick's poker!"

I mop the sweat from his forehead with a handkerchief.

"I don't like nobody touching me 'less I say so!" he snarls.

"I meant no harm. You're poorly and liable to a chill." I begin to wonder whether or not I hate this young Tartar for his lack of gratitude.

"A six-pounder blew my leg off. I guess no 'chill' is gonna do *me* any harm!"

I would be tender with him were it not for his anger, the contempt in which he plainly holds me, and the screaming of another poor bugger being partitioned by a surgeon's saw.

He points to my handkerchief. "Is your muckender clean?"

"Brand-new. I bring them for my boys, along with other treats."

"Give it here, then."

I hand him the item, and after blowing smut from his nose, he gives it back.

I want even this one to love me! Most in the wards do. They call me "Walt" or "Uncle" or "Father" and kiss my hands. Sometimes we kiss each other's mouths, lingeringly, as men will who grow fond.

"Does your wound pain you very much?" I hope I sound compassionate. (I feel disposed by his churlishness to touch his stump with a lighted cigar.)

"What do you think, old man?"

"Call me Walt," I tell him in a seductive voice.

My voice has been admired ever since the day I found it, praising Manifest Destiny on behalf of the Kings County Democratic Party. I was hardly more than a boy myself. I've become gray and vain. Still, I do care for these young men—I defy anyone to say otherwise.

"You got something of the redneck about you, Walter. You could be a nigger-breaker with them big hands of yours. I reckon what you are is a Johnny Reb spy come to finish us off with pocket handkerchiefs."

"My name is Walt." I give him a sly, prideful glance. "Walt Whitman."

The soldier, whose name I do not ask, scratches his bristled cheeks. He studies his fingernails. He digs underneath them with a matchstick. He pokes about in his ears with it. Clearly, my name means nothing to him. Though I'm disappointed, I won't be wounded by his slights. I understand his peevishness; I comprehend it. Pain and sorrow have broken him—the pain of the amputation and the sorrow for his lost leg. Who would not rage against the world—against God Almighty—having suffered such agony? And if he must rage against God and the kosmos, should I be exempted from his fury? Am I greater than they are that I should be spared his bitterness? Let him rage in his own words; let him, in his bitterness, ignore the sensibilities of the drumbeaters of salvation and the poets of democracy! Give him this day his daily curse, Oh, Lord.

"Is there something I can do for you?" I appear to

be looking at the wounded boy (he is one, for all his blustering), but it is Lewy Brown, the Marylander, who has caught my eye. He is lying on his cot, his lips compressed in an agony that he would keep to himself. His face, I think, resembles the lute player's in Caravaggio's *The Musicians*—or would do were it not for death's foretokens inscribed on it. "Would you like me to read to you? Perhaps one of my own poems?" I ask the peevish amputee, who is not worth a hair on my darling's head.

"Horseshit!" he replies while pinching his nostrils shut, so that I think he *has* heard of Walt Whitman and pretends otherwise in order to spite me.

I try not to let him see that he has hurt my feelings. I'm not ashamed to have an element of self-love in my nature. A man is many things; his character embraces contradictions that he himself cannot always resolve.

"Do you want to hear something from the paper?" I ask. "News of the newest slaughter and casualties?" I spoke, hoping to be cruel, and am aghast that I should have wished to be.

He yawns conspicuously. His teeth are bad. They sadden me more than his amputation. They speak of neglect and poverty. I would not kiss such a mouth.

He has turned his head away. Sleep, then, poor boy—sleep. In time, you, too, will love me.

I WORRY I SPEND WORDS AND FEELINGS too freely, and then I think neither of them is for hoarding. I become infatuated with this person or that one, according to my mood, or the ascendancy of the stars, conjunction of the planets, humors of the blood, phases of the moon, stages of the tide, the mesmeric currents. All things are electric, and bodies—those that are earthbound and those that are not of our Earth—are part of the vast corporeal sum. I add to it and subtract from it; I divide and multiply it. I affect outcomes; my death will also affect them. And the words I have uttered in anger or in love affect them also. My poems, which are the clearer part of me, will insinuate themselves into the consciousness of these States, and readers ages hence will know that I loved their predecessors without stint, as I love the men and women of the future without stint. None will say that I was niggling in my affections, nor will anyone accuse me of remaining aloof and keeping to myself the best tokens of affection, which are words.

How are we to understand men, if not by their words? I have heard them pray and speak tenderly, as well as revile, harangue, and revel in the rankest idioms of our native tongue. I know the dirty words and have tasted their foul syllables. They, too, are part of the lingo of a democratic people. They are the unconsecrated bread before the priest turns it into the body of Christ. They are the raw stuff of life before the poet turns it into song. Do you reckon that the wrathful Achilles was too refined to have called Ajax some vile name or, as he dressed his dear Patroclus's wound, he would not have cursed Zeus as "the father of thieves and whores"? I will do as Homer did for the Achaeans and the Trojans. Patroclus, whose wounds *I* dress, is not one Attic warrior, but ten thousand American soldiers fallen at the enemy's gates. I will remain their churchless missionary until this waste of men will have reached its inevitable conclusion: the suturing of our rent and bleeding Union. I leave the issue of emancipation and its consequences to Garrison, Whittier, and Stowe.

I sit awhile by the cot of a soldier of the Ninth New York Volunteer Infantry. I tell him that he will get well. He will convalesce and return to the Zouaves, whose bright red chasseur caps, sashes, and baggy trousers are so colorful against the short blue tunics of their uniforms. And the russet leather leggings are no less becoming to American men at arms than they are to the gallant French who fight against the Algerians for their empire's own manifest destiny.

"The bullet went through you without so much as a nick to your liver and lights. I'll bring needle and thread tomorrow," I say reassuringly. "To mend your jacket and blue shirt."

"Can you bring me a bag of boiled sweets?"

"And a cigar to enjoy, when you get up and about," I say.

One of the surgeons stops by the bedside, taps

the wounded man's chest, listens with an ear pressed close to it, peers down the man's throat, and examines the eyeballs, lifting one lid and then the other. I think he has been perfunctory. But when he stands and shakes his head, I know that, should I return tomorrow with needle and thread, the red tunic and baggy trousers, the red sash and the saucy chasseur cap will be gone, and their owner with them.

I take the young man's hand in mine. "Soon, you'll be with your regiment."

I think there is a grand regiment of the dead, which is enlisting men and boys, white and black, from every corner of the nation. See how the bargeman puts down his pole to take up the rifle and the sword. The mechanic likewise is putting by his file and lathe, the mason his plumb line, the carpenter his adze. The shoemaker leaves behind his hammer and last, the woodcutter the stand of yellow pines, the cooper his barrels and staves, the puddler his furnace, the smith his anvil and bellows. The Union has need of them, their clear eyes, native sagacity, and muscular arms. The carter, the teamster, the streetcar driver abandon their conveyances; henceforth, they will have armies and caissons to haul. The hostler closes the doors of the livery stable; soon he will curry the mounts of generals. The fireman exchanges his leather helmet for the blue forage cap of a Union infantryman to quench the fire of insurrection. The watchman deserts his post inside the warehouse, odorous with coffee beans, whale oil, or hops, to man a sentry post at some remote territorial fort that he will not desert. No longer will the waiter on tables in the finest establishment in Manhattan or the homeliest eatery in Duluth collect linen tablecloths stained by sumptuous dinners or greasy chops; henceforward, he will strip the sickbeds of soiled linen; he will gather bloody bandages, to be boiled in the steaming washtubs or burned. The war will be long and bitter, like the Arctic winter in which John Franklin perished. (The Union shall not perish.) It will gather up men and women and change them, so that not even their fathers, mothers, and sweethearts can recognize them. It will harvest young and old alike.

The dying man looks at me gratefully.

"I will bring paper and a stamp, and I'll help you write a letter to your father." Hereafter, I will sing of you—the glory and the grandeur of your brief life!

His father works in a livery stable near Fort Greene, in Brooklyn. I know it of old, though I do not recall ever having seen the father who gazed on his son with pride and affection when he first put on the Zouave uniform and marched off to hang Jeff Davis from a sour apple tree.

I stop by the cot of a man sick with dysentery. I do not flinch from the smell, nor do I turn away at the sight of the bloody stools.

"Dear boy," I say, bringing his hand to my lips.

He does not upbraid me for this intimacy, nor does he refuse my love. "You are one of mine," I tell him.

THIS MORNING I BEGIN WORK as a part-time copyist, under army paymaster Lyman Hapgood. In Washington, where I am notorious, no one else will hire me. Not even a recommendation from Ralph Waldo Emerson is sufficient against the prejudice of men like Secretary of the Treasury Chase, who defamed *L. of G.* as a "very bad book" and its author as "a decidedly disreputable person." Clerking will be dull, but without a salary, I must return to Brooklyn.

I walk through snow peppered with soot to the paymaster's, a brick building at the corner of West Fifteenth and L Streets. To save my boots, I keep to the ruts left behind by an artillery wagon. Inside the dismal office, which smells of wet wool and the rank odor of men, I stand at ease against a wall, horsehair peeping through the rough plaster, underneath a lithograph of the Sacramento River Massacre. Captain Frémont, imperturbable on horseback, prepares to fire his musket at a Wintun Indian. In the lithograph, which time and flies have stained, the hammer of his rifle will never fall and the ball never fly from its barrel, though the Wintun long ago passed on to his savage afterlife.

Curious, I watch a major unlock an iron strongbox,

while a corporal wearing a smutted pair of sleeve protectors sewn from what appears to have been a calico feed sack opens a ledger. Eighty-two negro infantrymen of Company B are to be paid this morning. They stand erect, as if Father Abraham himself were in the room, preparing to hand out cigars. The corporal dips his pen into the inkwell and calls each man to make his presence known. One by one, the men troop to the table and receive their pay from packages of five-, ten-, and twenty-five-cent pieces.

In the paymaster's office, the complications of war are a matter of arithmetic. In a stiff-backed book, the story of a man is told in the most elementary of narratives—an accounting in dollars and cents (thirteen dollars per month for a white private, seven for a black) until the final entry, when he is separated from the service or—not uncommon in wartime—his limb or his life. (The sum of all the dead recorded in history's gray ledgers would stagger and appall by an order of magnitude familiar to astronomers.) Whitman, are you to be one of Death's accountants who smile at the losses by which their master's kingdom is enlarged? What songs can come of so dire an office, save for dirges and threnodies?

When I found George among the living, I intended to return to Brooklyn. But how the others entreated me—not with words only but with their pitiable wounds! Because I could not abandon them, I came with them to Washington City. I stay for them, and will remain for those who will arrive at the Capital of Death, and I don't expect to leave here until the last of them have returned to their families, alive or coffined. To leave now would be a desertion in the face of what is loathsome, for that which we have a natural repugnance. I declare that nothing human repels me! I am not sickened by the sight of an oak shorn of limbs by a lightning bolt. Is a man any less than a tree that I would turn away from him when he is no longer whole?

At Falmouth field hospital, within sight and sound of the Rappahannock, I saw this:

> *Sight at daybreak*—in camp in front of the hospital tent on a stretcher, (three dead men lying,) each with a blanket spread over him—I lift up one and look at the young man's face, calm and yellow, —'tis strange!

What a poem lies waiting in those words! It is for you to write it, Walt Whitman, for none else can.

The snow begins to fall again. How glorious were the peaceable days when men would become, for an hour or two, boys packing snowballs in mittened hands or sleighing down white hills instead of slaying their fellows grown to manhood like themselves, in fields sprinkled red by the war priest's aspergillum!

I follow one of the negro soldiers outside. We stand a moment in the snow. I am curious and would ask him by what caprice of fate he has arrived at this place and whence did he come. The way the snow accumulates on the black wool of his pate and his wiry beard is also curious to me. He's a noble-looking fellow and not in the least repulsive. I take off my hat to show that the wet snow clots in my hair and beard as well as in his.

"My friend," I say, "were you and your comrades at Fredericksburg?"

"We were," he replies a little sulkily, I think.

"Was it very terrible?" I ask like an earnest schoolboy.

He looks at me as if I were a bug. I am several inches taller than he is, but I feel a pygmy in his presence. He shakes his head and goes.

You're a fool, Walt Whitman! Did you think that to stand bareheaded in the falling snow were misery enough to claim him as a comrade? What bitterness have you tasted other than that of a young writer's unfulfilled wish to see his fine words printed in *The Atlantic Monthly*? What hunger have you known? You have heard the groan in the gut when you've missed a meal, but none has ever escaped your lips because of a slaver's whip. When you have a toothache, you're given oil of clove; a cold on the stomach, paregoric; a fever, calomel. Wondrous preparations! (If only there were a simple one for a shattered femur!)

I am no longer young. I could have returned to my old haunts, instead of roughing it in Washington, which is not so picturesque as Zanzibar or Timbuktu. There will always be a chair for me in Pffaf's beer cellar on Broadway, a place on a Brooklyn rag, and a podium to stump for the Democratic Party. I could have kept well clear of events.

I was a firecracker on a bandstand. My words were incendiary. I strutted amid patriotic flags and bunting and on paper stages smelling of printer's ink—gasbagging for annexation, the Mexican War, James Polk, and the Long Island Democrats. I paraded and speechified, wearing a frock coat, a rakish hat, a loosely tied cravat, and—God save us from flâneurs and dandies!—stick on my arm and a gold pen in my pocket. (As if words could be enriched by the instrument of their inditing!) I was a young man to watch—the Beau Brummel of Brooklyn and the Bowery.

Paraded and speechified and little else! You've never engaged with an enemy except in newspaper squibs and lecture halls. Now you must engage with the bloody consequences of your high-flown words.

I am not without courage. Since my arrival in Washington, I have not flinched from the bloody consequences. When the surgeons cut and saw, I do not shut my eyes as flesh and bone are dropped into the pail. What a reek blood makes, and how my gut heaves! I bear it for the sake of the young men. For them, I utter other words than those I effused in the days of safety, in the heat of vain oratory fanned as if by the bellows of a pump organ. I will make verses suitable to the times. I will be the poet of war.

I see the negro infantryman who earlier rebuffed me. An ambulance has delivered him to Armory Square Hospital. He is laid on a cot among other black soldiers. His thick lips are parted, the tongue swollen in his mouth. He gapes like a fish pulled from the river. Blood trickles from the corner of his mouth, as if a hook were set there. He moans neither more nor less than other men. I stand in the doorway, looking at the terrible wounds. Not content to stand and look, I go inside to wrestle the angel of death. I throw him on my hip. Although I cannot beat him, I don't give up my boys to him without a fight. In my mind's eye, I see myself stroking the crisp, coiled hair of the wounded soldier. He does not rebuff me.

THE BATTLEFIELD WHOSE LENGTH and breadth I paced in Fredericksburg was quiet, save for the birds, the wind shaking the sourwood trees beside the river, and the river talking to itself. The passions of the combatants had been spent, the dead caught in the stillness of immortality, their fires quenched. Their blood, shed bravely or cravenly, had seeped into the earth. I had had no part in the affray, nor had I ever fought to the death. I have not pierced a man's gut with a bayonet; I've only spooned rice pudding down a sick man's gullet. I have not hefted a rifle and sighted along its barrel at a foe. Never have I watched a man crumple and fall or, the shot's having missed the mark, seen the dirt beside him jump or a chip of tree bark fly. Isaac Newton formulated the laws pertaining to the discharge of weapons; the flight of projectiles is predictable. Only men are not predictable, save that they perish according to eternal principles, and I—who am one of them—shall perish also, if not by shrapnel, ball, or bullet, then by some other means. Death is ingenious, and the ways by which the heart seizes and the lungs cease in their respiration are manifold.

In *Leaves of Grass*, I make much ado about me. I put myself at the center of great events and small doings alike. The lines of my verse are packed with *I*'s. Is there a sadder letter in the alphabet? See how austere and individual it appears, standing without an arm to wind about another, without a ligature to merge with another of its kind. Yet will I sing in praise of it: "I, ecstatic . . . !"

In the paymaster's office, the corporal is blotting ink on a ledger page, while the major locks the undisbursed money in the strongbox. A negro walks through the room, mopping the slush fallen from the soldiers' boots. Outside, a team of mules pulls a caisson up Pennsylvania Avenue toward Long Bridge. The caisson will cross the Potomac and climb into the Alexandria hills. Its load of ammunition will fortify one of the defensive forts around the city. The sound of its iron wheels is muffled by the packed snow of the street. I picture the driver, see how he holds the reins loosely. His head is sunk beneath his shoulder blades. The broad shoulders of his sack coat and the back of his neck are wet with snow. I've seen his like before, slumped on the hard seats of streetcars and omnibuses. Many times I kept the drivers company. They were good men filled with frank bonhomie. On a thoroughfare in New York or Brooklyn, I may have shared the reins with this same teamster, who is now heading toward Long Bridge to deliver his load.

Friend, might you be Broadway Jack, Yellow Joe, Balky Bill, or Old Elephant? You seem familiar. When I last saw you in Manhattan, you had no enemies, except the Plug Uglies, the Roach Guards, and the Dead Rabbits—villains who like to pull a stage driver from his seat into the road, where horses can trample him or wagon wheels crush him. Often I sat beside the hospital bed of one of my fallen comrades, and often did I linger at a freshly made grave. My eyes were full of tears. I don't dismiss the sentimental instinct any more than I do that of love or hate, if the love is true and the hate hot and dangerous. Sentimentality also has its place in the human amalgam. We are not all one thing or all another; we are the admixture of many things.

I lean against the wall and study the negro porter. I tell myself that the land that has a place for slaves and the owners of slaves has no place for freemen. I study the porter and think that he is not very much at variance with white men. I note the time on the New Haven clock: a quarter past one. I take note of the date on the calendar: January 4, 1863. I fear that the rebellion will not be so easily put down, as the bumptious North has promised the mothers, wives, and sweethearts who give away their boys and men to the ziggurat.

As the negro wrings the string mop into the pail, I ask him if he is glad the war has finally come. He makes no reply. Who is he that he should not answer me? Full of resentment, I make to tip the pail with the toe of my boot and send the gray water sprawling over the clean floor. But I am better than that. I am better than he is, who has not deigned to answer me.

I STOP OUTSIDE THE PRESIDENT'S HOUSE, hoping for a glimpse of Mr. Lincoln standing at one of the second-story windows. Although I disagree with his politics, I believe that the thread of my life and his is tangled in a skein that may well be impossible to unravel. Were it peacetime, I would knock on the front door and offer him a cigar and a pull at my flask. I'd shake his bony hand, and after we had become acquainted, I would put my arm around his narrow shoulders and call him "Abe." But the States and territories are not at peace, and a squadron of marines from the I Street barracks guards the front door.

What fate, I wonder, has brought him from Springfield to the "harrowing city"? Or was he drawn by a law of attraction not yet discovered? I reckon necessity carried him here, as it did me. I think that if there had been no secession, he would be in Illinois, reading law, as I would be in Brooklyn, reading Tennyson, Poe, Emerson, Tom Paine, and Frances Wright.

One day I will write your song, Mr. President.

I remember the first time I set eyes on you. You had stopped in New York on the way to Washington to begin your presidency. A rawboned country lawyer, you didn't strike me as a man capable of mucking out the Augean stable of the age. I climbed onto the roof of a streetcar in time to see you draw up to the Astor House in a shabby barouche. When you unlimbered from the coach and, on the pavement, stretched those long legs and stringy arms of yours, I thought I had seldom seen so ugly a man. No wonder your enemies called you "Ape" Lincoln. Lanky, your face lined and tanned like an old leather boot, you seemed a caricature of yourself. Then you tipped back your stovepipe, pushed up the ends of your clawhammer coat, and faced the crowd that had brought Broadway to a halt. Most were hostile; New York is a nest of Copperheads. As you looked us over, you were neither afraid nor antagonistic. You were curious, as I would have been curious in your place.

I will write your song, I said to myself. Pray God it does not mourn.

I walk down West Fifteenth to the canal, which was built as a water route across the city, connecting the Anacostia River with Tiber Creek and the "Grand Old Ditch" running beside the Potomac to Cumberland, Maryland. Instead of barges, the canal carries sewage and contributes its stink to that of the pigsties and marshes. I don't need the foul channel to remind me of our corporeal nature. In the casualty wards, my hands root in it, and my boot soles slip on it if the attendant has not yet mopped the floor. Sometimes I walk along the canal—not, as I said, to purge my lungs of the atoms of corruption with fresh air, for there is none in its vicinity, but at the behest of an inner voice. I let it have its say. I don't begrudge my compulsions; they, too, are an aspect of my character. And so it is that I find myself perambulating beside the fetid, stagnating channel.

A man catches up to me. He puts a gloved hand on my elbow. I recognize him as one of the newspapermen who are everywhere in the city. They are billeted for the duration, as am I. He is wearing a checkered suit. His gloves are lavender; his cravat is garish. I like him for the insolence of his clothes. His refusal to be seen à la mode is wonderful to me. He pushes his "crusher" up from his broad forehead, revealing a wave of dark hair.

"Washington is a fine city for Hottentots," he

says in the ironic way of the inky tribe, to which I belonged.

"It's not meant for show." I find myself wanting to defend the people's city even here by the noxious canal, whose odor is that of a shambles. "It's the seat of our democracy."

"They ought to have kept it in Philadelphia. Washington is no better than a flea circus."

The suggestion sets me to scratching. My performance amuses him.

"Philadelphia is a pleasant town," I say, allowing him that much. "Though nothing beats Manhattan—except, maybe, Brooklyn."

"New York is all right for rich men, whores, and Hebrew cigar rollers."

I don't care to acknowledge his invidious remark, howsoever I may agree with it.

"Speaking of cigars, I have a box of Havanas in my room. Would you care to try one? I also have a tipple for the tipplers."

I smile, and he takes my arm.

"Edward Oakes," he says, giving me his other hand to shake.

"Walt Whitman," I say, feeling, as always, a thrill to hear my name pronounced. It is a proper name for a man of the people and the poet of democratic vistas.

We walk north to Pennsylvania Avenue. Next door to the Kirkwood House, I stop at Miller's and buy a bag of horehound drops for Corporal Tawes, who is fond of the sweet. We continue on to the Willard Hotel, a block east of the President's House. I follow Oakes up the staircase to his room, feeling a bridegroom's nervousness. I move the room's only chair to the window and look out on the red sandstone towers of the Smithsonian—a bequest to the United States, given by one of its admirers, James Smithson of Great Britain, delivered in 105 canvas sacks containing 104,960 gold sovereigns. How wonderful the world of facts! Each is a nail in the mouth of a carpenter, ready to be hammered home. Each is a morsel of reality—materialism first and last imbuing. (No facts without words. No reality, either.)

I choose a cigar from the box. I sniff its length like a connoisseur. I rub it between my fingers to judge its freshness. I refuse the small scissors Oakes offers and bite off the end like a country clod. I smile at the recollection of the day Henry Thoreau visited me in my attic room on Classon Avenue in Brooklyn. For all his disdain for convention, he turned up his nose at the untidiness of my establishment.

"Do you approve?" asks Oakes, cigar smoke leaking between his bearded lips.

"The Cuban soil produces excellent tobacco," I say, holding my cigar at arm's length and admiring it judiciously. "It draws beautifully."

"We'll have her someday!" declares Oakes with unexpected vehemence.

"Have what?"

"Cuba! Mark my word, we'll take her from the *zambos* and run up the Stars and Stripes above Morro Castle. It's our destiny! We're the new colossus, and by God, we will bestride the hemisphere!"

I have held the same opinion and declaimed it in newspaper columns and from reviewing stands, but to hear it put so baldly by this gent makes me squirm.

Oakes opens a bottle of sherry and fills a tumbler.

"No whiskey?" I ask, contemptuous of this genteel tipple.

"We like our sherry in Philadelphia," he replies smugly. The way he smacks his lips brings to mind Fortunato in Edgar Poe's delicious tale "The Cask of Amontillado."

Refusing the glass, I take the bottle and pour the contents down my neck.

"You are a Democrat," he says, showing his teeth.

I agree with him, my eyes sparkling with malice.

"You know, I've heard of you. You're the fellow who wrote an immoral book." Before I can protest, he exclaims, "Good for you, Whitman!"

To accept his praise would be to agree that *L. of G.* is immoral. I debate the matter with myself and then let it go. Instead, I ask him if he has read it.

"I've got no appetite for poems, unless they're comical. Have you read Lowell's *The Biglow Papers*? Stick out your ears, Walt." He recites "The Pious Editor's Creed" from memory and makes a hash of its colloquialisms:

> I du believe in Freedom's cause,
> Ez fur away ez Paris is;
> I love to see her stick her claws
> In them infarnal Pharisees;
> It's wal enough agin a king
> To dror resolves an' triggers—
> But libbaty's a kind o' thing
> Thet don't agree with niggers.

"I don't care for the word," I say with a sniff of disapproval.

"*Niggers?* Say, you ain't an abolitionist, are you? It's their mealy mouths that got us into this fix."

"I am the poet of slaves and of the masters of slaves."

"Walter, you surprise me! You get your back up at a word you can hear spoken in a parsonage, yet you think nothing of putting the word *fuck* into your poetry!"

"Oakes, if you'd read it, you would know that's not the case."

"I beg your pardon. I didn't mean to touch a nerve. Fellow told me it was. Say, why don't I send the boy to buy us a quart? What do you say to that, Walt Whitman?"

I open the window and take a draught of cold air. I look into Fourteenth Street, where a company of infantry is riding toward Long Bridge, beyond which hazards await them like snares set out by boys to catch birds.

He opens his wallet and spills greenbacks onto the bed. "What about it?"

I put on my coat and hat.

"No need for you to go—I'll send the boy."

"The air is bad in here."

"It's Washington!"

I start for the door.

"Stay awhile," he entreats. "I'll get you some rye whiskey. Later on, I'll treat you to a chop. Willard's has a first-class *table d'hôte.*"

He bungles the French as badly as he did James Russell Lowell's attempt at American dialect. Ordinarily, I would enjoy hearing one of the languages of Europe mangled. At this moment, however, I feel only contempt for Oakes, his checkered trousers, and his yellow shoes.

I leave without a word in parting.

"Well, if that don't take the rag off the bush!" he says in wonderment as I close the door behind me.

I ARRIVE TOO LATE TO GIVE the young corporal his sweets. As I approach the cot, an army chaplain is commending his soul to God. I take off my hat and attend to the words:

> Thou hast now taken him to Thyself.
> Comfort us who remain; help us to the
> end of life patiently to bear its burdens
> and trials; and when our last hour shall

come, be Thou the strength of our heart
and our portion forever.

The chaplain closes his book.

"You're with the Christian Commission," he says,
as if to clarify my presence.

"I am."

"It's a goddamn shame to see so many young men
taken!"

I do not react to his oath. Blasphemy has nothing to do with me. Neither does decorum nor piety. I
leave them to others to fuss over. My business is with
men and the words by which they are known.

He rises to his full height and looks defiantly at
me. I return his gaze with equal defiance. I refuse to
be made a party to anyone's war with God, for in his
eyes, this man has the look of Jacob wrestling with
the angel. The chaplain seems to repent of his haugh-
tiness. He bends a little the ramrod of his back. He
relaxes the muscles of his jaws, so that his bearded
lips part. I think that he will smile at me, but he
frowns instead. "Forgive me," he mutters.

I don't find it strange to be asked for my forgiveness by a parson. Already this war has stood the
world on its head. Why shouldn't the relationship of
one of God's men and me also be stood on its head?

We leave the ward together. I reckon this man
is worth knowing. I think that he carries a burden
that—at a time when nearly everyone alive shoulders a weight of care—is heavier than that borne

by most others. He asks for the pleasure of buying me a drink. I don't find it strange that he should. Liquor is a consolation for anyone who feels lonely and afraid. An army chaplain has as much reason to feel frightened and alone as the next man. War can cause decorous men to behave in ways that they would have considered unthinkable before every damn thing went to hell.

The chaplain and I go to a tavern near Lafayette Square and drink to each other's health.

"In Mexico, I drank the fermented sap of the maguey plant," he says. "It's potent. It can overcome a man before he realizes; it can send him into oblivion."

I would like to ask him if God can be found in oblivion, but I don't.

He tells me about his service as a chaplain in Winfield Scott's army during the Mexican-American War. He was at Chapultepec Castle when Colonel Harney oversaw the hanging of the Patricios, and also in Huamantla when Lane's Texas Rangers burned and looted the town to avenge the death of Sam Walker. He tells me that he was caught in the thigh by one of General Rea's lancers at Galaxara Pass. He relates his story without flourishes or vainglory. Nor does he speak as a penitent would to ease a tormented conscience. In the confessional of the barroom, darkness seeping in from the cold night beyond the frosted windowpanes, he speaks like someone impelled to recite his own history, incredulous that it should already be so various.

I would guess that Captain Winter—his given name is Robert—is in his thirties, although he has the raddled appearance of someone much older. He is as irreligious a man of God as I have yet to encounter. It is not only the coarseness of his speech, which can be explained by association with rough soldiers, but also his apparent indifference to the Deity. He does not fear God. He believes a man must act even if he lacks all conviction. John Brown instructed him in that dubious principle the night before he was hanged for the business at Harper's Ferry. Winter had been ordered by Robert E. Lee—a lieutenant colonel in the U.S. Army at the time—to give Brown the comforts of his savior. Winter did as he was told. I suspect those comforts are warm beer to the men in my keeping.

"Do I shock you?" he asks when he has finished his speech, for so his recitation seemed.

"Not much," I say. "I've known all kinds of men."

"That's just what I'd expect of the poet of *Leaves of Grass*."

"You know me?" I ask, astonished.

"I recognized you from the engraving on the frontispiece."

"Did you bother to read my book?"

"I did. I like how you sing, even if I don't believe a word of the song."

I resist the temptation to be peevish.

"I took an interest in poetry after becoming acquainted with Emily Dickinson. There's no reason that you should have heard of her, though she's an extraordinary poet. I have the word of those equipped to judge such matters. I'm only a soldier."

"Of the Lord or of General McClellan?" The men call him "Young Napoleon." I consider him a prig better suited to a picnic ground than a battlefield.

Winter smiles—cunningly, I think—but does not reply.

"And the lady—is she still living?" I ask him.

"Yes, if you can call it that. Miss Dickinson is famous as a recluse in Amherst, a ghostly figure in white glimpsed occasionally through the windows of her Homestead. I have one of her verses tucked in my wallet. They manage to find me wherever I'm posted. Shall I read it?"

"By all means," I say, though I am wary of the effusions of lady poets.

Winter reads from a scrap of paper in a manly voice that does not mince or caper:

> To fill a Gap
> Insert the Thing that caused it—
> Block it up
> With Other—and 'twill yawn the
>   more—
> You cannot solder an Abyss
> With Air.

"It's not clear to me what she means to say."

"Nor to me, but it is her way. She was discovered —I suppose the word is apt in this case—by Thomas Wentworth Higginson, a captain in the Fifty-first Massachusetts Infantry."

"I know Higginson. Miss Dickinson is lucky not to have had her work defamed. He said in public that my chief mistake in writing *Leaves of Grass* is not that I wrote it but that I did not burn it afterward."

Winter guffaws, and for an instant, I hate both him and Higginson, a fatuous critic and a self-styled poet.

"I always supposed the man was an ass!" says Winter, redeeming himself in my eyes.

"Where is your home, Captain?"

"In my Father's mansion, there are many rooms." Seeing my puzzlement, he explains. "In that I owe filial obedience to a superior, the army is my father, and his mansion is the States and territories." He scratches his nose a moment, then says, "I doubt the Almighty will welcome me to His."

"You endorse, then, the nation's destiny."

"I acknowledge the fact that the nation has a ravenous appetite for acreage."

Unwilling to spoil the evening with an argument, I signal the barkeep to fill our empty glasses. Winter and I drink quietly. Other voices, previously subsumed beneath our conversation, become louder and more insistent. I listen to a Copperhead at a table behind me reading from an editorial in *The Salem Advocate,* published in Lincoln's own Illinois:

> . . . he is no more capable of becoming a statesman, nay, even a moderate one, than the braying ass can become a noble lion. People now marvel how it came to pass that Mr. Lincoln should have been selected as the representative man of any party. His weak, wishy-washy, namby-pamby efforts, imbecile in matter, disgusting in manner, have made us the laughing stock of the whole world.

A second man concurs in the scurrilous opinion. He mocks the president, calling him a "yahoo" and "gorilla." He reviles him as a coward for having disguised himself in a soft hat, muffler, and bobtailed coat to arrive unnoticed in Washington to begin his presidency. At the Harrisburg, Pennsylvania, depot, he had been informed that an attempt would be made on his life that night. Lincoln had put himself in jeopardy by insisting that he ride in an ordinary sleeper car instead of a private train with a military escort. My own *Brooklyn Eagle* lampooned him in "Mr. Lincoln's Flight by Moonlight Alone" and declared him deserving of "the deepest disgrace that the crushing indignation of a whole people can inflict." The *New-York Tribune* opined that "Mr.

Lincoln may live a hundred years without having so good a chance to die."

"If ever a Caesar deserves a Brutus, Lincoln is that man!" the first man sneers.

I can bear it no longer. Noisily, I push back my chair, and the two backbiters turn their heads toward me. They have the look of disappointed office seekers or men whose businesses will be ruined by a civil war. I take each of them by the throat. They sputter in helpless rage in my clutches. They don't understand why they are being molested; they cannot guess the reason for my anger.

"I'd rather not soil my hands on you two ass-wipers, but I fear I'm about to choke the life out of both of you!"

My fury is aimed partly at myself for deriding Lincoln and the Republican Party in the weeks before his election. I am a Democrat; like Jefferson and Andrew Jackson, I fear a strong federal government. I distrust the centralization of power. I am for the States—let them govern themselves. I am for the individual—let each man look to his own self-rule. But I will not stand to hear the president of the United States abused. He is for the Union, and I, too, am for it. In this, we agree.

The barkeep is behind me. He is a burly man, larger than I, who am six feet tall. He is wide across the shoulders. His fists are like two ruddy hams. He has me by the throat, as I have the two villains by theirs. I feel myself weakening my hold on them. I feel myself growing faint as the blood leaves my head. A commotion is heard behind me, followed by a splintering noise. The barkeep's hands are no longer at my throat. I turn in time to see him fall, his scalp drizzling blood through his thin, greasy hair. Captain Winter holds a broken chair. His face is triumphant; his eyes sparkle with boyish excitement. Unhurried, he leads me by the arm into the street, where I am revived by the night air.

"There'll be hell to pay," I tell him.

"Then they can dun the Devil, because tomorrow I'll be with Hooker in Virginia."

He offers me an ironic salute in farewell. I tip my hat and wish him "Godspeed."

"God has no say in the matter," he replies archly. "I'm at the mercy of the Army of the Potomac and the Washington and Alexandria Railroad."

Captain, I do not think we shall meet again.

I stop awhile in Lafayette Square. The windows are lighted in the President's House. In my mind's eye, I see Lincoln pacing the galleries. Troubled and alone, he is wrapped in his old shawl against the cold. I feel myself tremble both in dread and pity. I don't know if he will be a great president and commander in chief. He is untried and unannealed, and the occasion to which he has risen is dire.

I wanted to tell the captain of a July Fourth long ago when the Marquis de Lafayette had picked me up and set me safely down again at an excavation on the corner of Cranberry and Henry Streets in Brooklyn. He had arrived in a yellow coach to lay the cornerstone for the Apprentices' Library building. I had been one of the children chosen to stand beside him. He pressed me lovingly to his breast. He may have even kissed me. I like to think that he did. I have always believed that I was somehow marked by the occasion—that my name was entered in a ledger that has nothing to do with dollars and cents.

I search the sky, hoping to see a comet. Tonight the stars seem wary of Earth; their fires are stoked to keep the race of men at bay. We are a dangerous species, Walt, and the stars are right to keep their distance.

I TAKE DOWN THE WORDS of a corporal of marines gravely injured by a torpedo placed in the coal bunker of a Union gunboat by a Confederate agent during Burnside's blockade of the Outer Banks at Roanoke Island. His charred hands are swathed in bandages. The surgeons have done all they can. I wonder if he will ever hold the hand of a sweetheart or close the eyes of his father, mother, or a beloved friend the moment he passes from the quick to the dead. It is only an instant, that passage, but it shatters worlds.

January 6, 1863

Dear Mother,

A friend is writing this, as I burned my hand on a hot stove. It will soon be right again. I am fine and enjoying the sights. I saw Mr. Lincoln get out of his buggy and go into the President's House. He is tall, like everyone says, and his stovepipe makes him look even taller. I am eating well, and have put on weight.

I hope you and Father and the two girls are fine. Tell them I am hoping to see them soon as this war is over with. I miss your rhubarb pie and would give a month of army pay to have a slice. Write to me when you can in care of Armory Square Hospital, Ward K, District of Columbia.

Your loving son,
Ethan

I've written twoscore of such letters since my arrival in Washington.

"Is there anything else you need, Ethan?" I look at the gaunt face and picture it gone red after a day's larking in the sun or flushed by the exertion of rowing in the meadows of the bay. I drive out the thought of the rouge that will one day color his cheeks and mine when we are laid out and waiting for what comes next. "I've an apple in my pocket with your name on it."

"Thank you kindly, Walt, but I'm feeling puny."

"Close your eyes, then, and get some sleep."

He closes them, and I wonder if I will see them open again. It is only his hands, Walt, not his vitals! With help, a man can get along just fine without his hands.

"Superintendent Dix wants a word with you, Whitman," says a ward attendant. He wears the bespattered apron of his trade and smokes to keep the stink of gangrene and dysentery from getting up his nose.

I follow him, dreading an interview with "Dragon" Dix, superintendent of nurses for the Union army. She is as formidable as her handle suggests, and her stern voice can make captains quake. She cares much for the men, I will give her that, although I think she has no love for me.

Crossing the armory mall, I'm entranced by the sight of white sheets bellying in a wind that pulls the wash lines taut; they have been hung out to dry under the thin January sun. Seeing them, I recall standing on Vinegar Hill to watch the frigates sail down the East River from the Brooklyn Navy Yard, making for Sandy Hook and the Atlantic Ocean. Would that I were there now, sauntering with one of my camerados!

No, Walt, you are where you need to be, and also wish to be.

Many a soldier's loving arms about this
neck have cross'd and rested,
Many a soldier's kiss dwells on these
bearded lips.

In the present conflict, many men will be taken out of their lives; many women also. *Leaves of Grass* is the book in which convulsions of great nations will be recorded, as well as the tremors that pass unregarded through the least of us—aye, even the worst of us. I will not let them pass without pausing to regard them. They, too, shall have a place in the universal history of our kind.

At a rolltop desk, Dorothea Dix sits as ramrod straight as Robert E. Lee does his horse. She is writing—I doubt it's a poem. She has more important things to occupy her mind. One of them is a swaggering poet named Walt Whitman, who stands before her, wearing a wine-colored suit and a necktie. He's quite the swell! Superintendent Dix lets me stew as she blots the ink dry before swiveling around to glare at me. The chair creaks like Methuselah's old bones. I must cut a poor figure in my finery. (I can change my clothes but not my character.)

"Mr. Whitman," she says curtly.

"I am he." I don't remove my hat; I give a fillip to the brim. Insolence is becoming to the poet of democracy and as good a way as any to beard the dragon in her den.

"Are you not a delegate of the U.S. Christian Commission?"

"I plead guilty and await sentencing." Walt, you're in a droll mood today!

"It has been brought to my attention that you use profane language in the wards."

"I speak the language of men, Superintendent Dix."

"That may be, Mr. Whitman, but it is not a language I wish to hear in Armory Square or any other hospital in my charge."

"To hear it is a comfort to my boys." It reminds them of their lost innocence.

"They're not boys, and they are certainly not yours!"

"I beg your pardon, ma'am. It's only a manner of speaking."

"I was told you refuse to distribute certain tracts that the Sanitary Commission produces for the benefit of the patients, and at great expense."

"I feared that *The Dangers of Dancing* would be a painful reminder to some of their former gaiety."

"Are you being impertinent, Mr. Whitman?"

"Not at all, Nurse Dix. I thought the tract superfluous in view of their present condition." Oh, do not let her see me smirk!

"Their *spiritual* condition also concerns us, Mr. Whitman. 'Better to be maimed or halt in life than to be cast into hellfire.'"

Where they hotfoot it but do not dance—no, not even a *paso doble* with the Devil.

She regards me with a measure of hostility. "Several nurses have spoken against you."

Not Nurse Wright! Of all the medical staff, she seems to understand the healing power of magnetic love.

"Nurse Hawley has written to her husband, the brigadier general. I saw the letter. She refers to you as 'that *odious* Walt Whitman.'" The word stings. "She complains that you 'talk evil and unbelief' to the men. She declares that she 'would rather see the evil one himself—at least if he had horns and hooves'—in her ward. Nurse Akin is also concerned by your 'peculiar interest in our soldier boys.'"

I serve the Dragon her own words to eat: "They are not boys, and they are certainly not hers!"

Dix ignores the gibe. "And your 'peculiar interest'—what of that?"

"Yes, Miss Dix, I do have a peculiar interest in helping them to recover what they can of their former selves and, for those past help, to give them whatever consolation I can."

"You make Nurse Akin's thumbs prick, Mr. Whitman!" Dix bites her lower lip. I watch a flush climb up her neck from her starched white collar. She would be a pretty woman were she to unclench her jaw.

"Whatever can she mean by pricking thumbs?"

"You're too friendly with the patients, Mr. Whitman!"

"I should hope to be their friend! Friendship and a few treats—which I purchase with my own scant funds—is all I can give them. I wish I had your nursing skill, Miss Dix. You give them more than an apple or a bag of sweets. My hat is off to you!" I say, keeping mine on.

I hold her gaze a moment. I expect she is unsure whether or not I am ragging her. She concludes the interview with an admonition: "You must rein in your affections, Mr. Whitman, for your own good."

Strolling by the canal, I review the scene in my mind and feel ashamed. Miss Dix has an army of sick and wounded men in her keeping. She doesn't need to contend with a smart aleck. I've heard she's an advocate for the insane. God speed her in that good cause, since my brother Jesse's syphilis will likely earn him a bed and a *camisole de force* in the Kings County Lunatic Asylum. (God bless the French for giving us the straitjacket, the guillotine, and the books of the Marquis de Sade!) How various is the world and how bewildering in its variety!

ON PENNSYLVANIA AVENUE, the horses emerge from darkness into a ring of gaslight before once more plodding into obscurity. I keep company with Peter Doyle, a conductor on the Georgetown–Navy

Yard streetcar, as he makes the last trip of the day. Peter and I understand each other. When the car has emptied of passengers (except as might be a drink-fuddled sailor or two returning to their ship), I will take his hand, or he mine. No words need pass our lips. Words are superfluous in the electric atmosphere. It is enough to listen to the heavy hoofbeats of the weary horses. The driver sits quietly on his box, a loaded pistol beside him. Cutthroats, deserters, spies, swindlers, and scamperers from ruined reputations and enterprises prowl the capital by night. It's a pokerish business to go among them, alone and unarmed. Fearing none, I go when and where I like. I do not look for trouble; neither will I let any man molest me. I am as expert with a knife as any Bowery Boy or East River tramp.

A Patent Office clerk and a man with a worried look got off earlier at Virginia Avenue to pursue their solitary ways. Maybe a son was wounded at Fredericksburg or lost in the Shenandoah Valley after being harassed by Stonewall Jackson's men. It may be that the worried man himself has been conscripted or is hopelessly entangled in adultery. I imagine all. I am a stranger to nothing that passes between men or between men and women. What they purpose, I purpose; what they do, I do also. What black-robed judges deem unlawful and starched churchmen condemn as sin are, for me, neither. I'm not for robbery, arson, murder, treason, or betrayal. I am for the body, as God must be for the body, or He would have chosen another habitation for the soul. The souls of men and women are His. I am for the radiant transactions of the flesh. No shame attaches to my forty-three years on this Earth.

At the Navy Yard, I shake the besotted sailors awake, not as a stern father does a "lazy" son or a master a "good-for-nothing" apprentice, but tenderly, as a mother does the apple of her eye. I think of Harriet Wright, whom the boys in the wards love. I have seen her blow upon the hectic cheek of a wounded soldier to bring him softly to his senses. The women who wash the bodies of men, who clean and dress the putrid wounds, are radiant as the Virgin glowing in the stained glass of St. Patrick's Cathedral. Nurse Akin and Nurse Hawley—they, too, are superb, despite the contempt they show me. Their contempt can neither shorten nor lengthen my days, so why should it concern me?

I help the two sailors from the car. They stand swaying in the street. They lean against each other so as not to fall. The black neckerchief of one is unknotted, and I knot it for him. I admire the muscles of his neck—like hawsers, I think. The other man holds his cap, and I set it on his head at the regulation angle. I smooth the rumpled tar flaps on the backs of their blouses. They are fine fellows, regardless of the vomit on their shoes. They give me a friendly salute and stagger off toward their ship. I recall the company of U.S. Colored Troops assembled in the paymaster's office. They were manly enough, bright enough, looked as if they had the soldier stuff in them, but I think that they will never be amalgamated. They will always have more of Ethiopia in them than of the States. Yet they do not shirk and have acquitted themselves well in battle. As such, they belong in the poem of democracy, for which many will perish.

I recall a letter that I penned for Roland Brecht. I picture his mother as her fearful gaze sweeps over the words. Her tears tremble at the ends of her fine lashes, ready to fall onto the creased paper. In time, it will be worn thin with folding and unfolding. The letter will have worn to pieces before she has worn out her grief. For a mother, there is no end to mourning. Roland's mother will not hold her son on her lap; she is not the Madonna, and her son is not the Son of Man.

> O this is not our son's writing, yet his
>   name is sign'd,
> O a strange hand writes for our dear
>   son, O stricken mother's soul!

Rows of manly faces appear to my mind's eye. The eyes in many of the faces have closed and will not open again. The bodies will be taken downstairs to the dead house. The beds will be stripped of their sheets. The sheets will be scrubbed with carbolic soap and hung up to dry.

The driver is urging the horses into the car barn. The leather reins snapping against their backs are unnecessary; so, too, is the clicking of his tongue. The horses are spent and long for their stalls and fodder.

"I see far worse sights than the average soldier does," I tell Pete, and am shocked to hear a secret pride in my voice.

"I know that, Walt."

Pete and I are standing by the dashboard, which shields passengers from mud flung backward by the horses' hooves. (Oh, for a contrivance to keep the mud of reviewers from spattering one's honest pages with their self-important critiques!)

"Pete, I can't help thinking that behind each casualty is a coon."

"I have no argument with them," he replies, while the driver undresses the horses of their tack.

"In that they are men, they are my brothers. But there's something in the constitution of the negro's mind that unfits him for emancipation. No race can ever remain slaves if they have it in them to become free. Why did the slave ships go to Africa only?"

Pete turns his head away and spits. Whether he does so because he agrees with me or has nothing more to say on the subject, I don't know. Maybe he is just bringing up what rowdies call an "oyster." I am not offended by the lack of delicacy in his manner.

"My brother George said, 'We'll have to win the war before we can free them.'"

"That's a fact," says Pete.

"I worry the cost may be too high."

"You've got the hospital stink up your nose, Walt. Let's you and me have a smoke and throw some liquor down our necks."

We walk past the silent Navy Yard and step into one of the barrooms near the river. The Anacostia is blacker than the night sky, which tonight is faintly illumined. The moon is low in the west. The enemy in its thousands and tens of thousands is bathing in its silvery light. They also pray for deliverance. Time will tell which side of the issue He favors, unless the God of the North is different from Him of the South. Perhaps the Ancient of Days is black and will deliver His people out of bondage. Theirs is a far older race than ours, and He may have struck off His likeness onto them. (Unproven, there may be no God at all.) I'm not a religious enthusiast; I am for men and women, religious and irreligious alike. I have no enemies, save Nurse Hawley and Nurse Akin.

By the oil lamp, I study Pete Doyle's boyish face. A rash has come out on it; he frets that he has syphilis. Because he fears it, the Irish Catholic strain has come out strong. I listen to him bewail his weakness for the flesh, which, he says, will send him to perdition. At such times, I consider him pathetic and swear to be rid of him. But I am infatuated by his youth, pretty face, and slender figure. I told him that I'd take a room outside Washington for us, where I would root out the thing. I told him I would build him a "tabernacle" in which to squat amid fumes given up by boiling mercury—a treatment favored by old-world syphilitics. But Peter only pouted.

Tonight, however, he is jolly and contented to be sitting near me. He puts his hand on my knee and looks at me sweetly. I am twice his age, and those who see us loafing by the putrid canal or in the car barn, waiting to set out on one of our nocturnal travels across the city, would likely mistake us for a father and his son. He is very like a son to me, and also like a lover. I forgive him everything.

I find it pleasant to be unencumbered in a barroom late at night with my boy. It is a low haunt frequented by sailors, merchantmen, dock porters, and stevedores. If I were to lean across the table and stroke Pete's light-colored hair, none would give a damn. I could buss him on the lips for all the notice anybody would take. Men who are more often at sea than on land—they, too, enjoy the athletic love of which I sing in *Leaves*.

Pete is relating a humorous tale. Satisfied to watch his lips part, revealing a row of even teeth, I do not attend to his words. Although he is an illiterate and his opinions are dubious, he has the charm of his race, and I will often hang upon his every word. But tonight it is enough for me to watch his lips.

"I went to the Patent Office this morning," I tell him now that his lips have been given to a cigar. "It's being used as a hospital. Cots jam the lobby and are set among the display cases in the galleries. It's the same in the Capitol Building. I can imagine a time when Washington will be inhabited only by sick and wounded boys. They'll nurse themselves, as people did in the old plague days, when even the doctors and apothecaries were struck down. The night sky will be set ablaze by a conflagration of soiled sheets and pillowcases, bandages and handkerchiefs. The town—what's that line of Melville's?—will be taken over by rats."

"I get sick and tired of hearing about your sick and wounded boys!" Doyle snarls as he touches the rash on his face.

I have reminded him of his fear, but I find myself resentful of his egotism. I think of poor Lewy Brown, who bravely bears his suffering.

"The city is awash in casualties—fifty thousand on the books so far this year." Oh, those tall gray ledgers! Their leaves are so very different from my own.

He shrugs, sets the rank cigar on a plate, and swallows his glass of rum in one go.

Perversity bids me continue to irk him. "It's not something to be shrugged at, Peter."

"Old man, you are boring me to death."

He glances at a muscular lout I've seen carrying sacks out of the holds of ships. His face wears the stupefied expression of an ox waiting for the sledgehammer to fall. He may be feebleminded or merely soaked in drink, but I see nothing in him to admire. Evidently, Pete finds him attractive, unless he hopes to rile me. "I wonder if that great fellow sitting by himself would like some company." Like a lovesick swain, I reach for Pete's hand and spill my glass of beer. Now I am the pathetic one. Sensing his triumph, which is that of youth over an aged man's desire, Pete smiles serenely.

"You're a swine!" I say.

He snorts like one. How vulgar, I think, how very childish!

He must see the disapproval on my face, because he stands and lurches toward the other man's table. I put my hand on his arm to stay him. His face reveals a conceit I find intolerable.

"Forgive me," I say, regardless of my anger. To love another is to be at his mercy. Only when one is too old or sick to love is one finally disenthralled.

Pete resumes his seat. He presses my hand to his cheek. He has beaten me and can be magnanimous. The barkeep wipes the wet table with his towel. He fills my empty glass with beer. Pete indicates his cup. The barkeep brings the square bottle of rum and pours. Pete and I lock arms and drink, gazing into each other's eyes.

Pete, my darling!

"Do you remember the night we met?" I ask.

"You were the only passenger. It was a lonely night, so I thought I would speak to you. Something in me made me do it. We were familiar at once—I put my hand on your knee—we understood."

What foolishness is this, Walt—tears?

"The rims of your eyes are very pink." He means no offense, and I am not offended.

His eyes betray his dissipation. I think of the eyes of the soldiers in the wards: weary eyes, anguished, empty, staring, perplexed, angry, hurt eyes. Some nights I dream of them. I wake in a cold sweat and am afraid to fall back to sleep.

Pete has been telling me about a 380-pound Union soldier put on exhibition at Richmond Military Prison. Although my thoughts had wandered before Pete reached the end of the joke, I chuckle. I see that he is disappointed. This time, I give a belly laugh. Beaming, he tilts his chair back on two legs against the wall. The "stingy brim" of his porkpie hat rises comically from his brow. He stuffs his hands into his coat pocket. I laugh in earnest. The others in the room look at us over the tops of their schooners of beer.

"Your turn, old man."

"Nothing comes to mind," I say, wishing I were tucked up in bed for the night.

"Give us some Shakespeare, then."

I have often regaled my comrades by reciting lines from the Bard, who, in my opinion, is the only other poet worthy of the name.

"Tomorrow," I say, hoping to put Pete off. With

a little encouragement, I would fall into the arms of Morpheus and let him have his way with me.

"I know that one!" he says. "Tomorrow, tomorrow, tomorrow . . . How does it go?"

I sigh and begin:

> Tomorrow, and tomorrow, and
>   tomorrow,
> Creeps in this petty pace from day to
>   day,
> To the last syllable of recorded time;
> And all our yesterdays have lighted fools
> The way to dusty death.

Pete drums the tabletop with his hands. Three blue jackets, hauled up from the deeps of insobriety by my recitation, clap. A merchantman nods in approval. By the words on his cap, I know him to be a foreigner.

"I know this play," he says. "*Makbet.*" He recites the speech in Polish, simply, as if he has taken to heart Hamlet's advice to the players against sawing the air and tearing a passion to tatters, as I am wont to do when carried away by gusts of eloquence.

"Are you surprised, mister? I have read all the tragedies in Polish and English."

I look at him as one would at a diamond set in a pile of filth. "Dear man, you take my breath away!"

He thanks me "very much."

"Will you drink with us?" I ask him.

"It is my honor." He brings his chair to our table. The veins stand out on his muscled forearms where the sleeves have been rolled up. He is blond and blue-eyed. His gaze is frank. He is in robust condition—a young man whom I would guess to be in his early thirties. Here, Walt, is another you could love.

"Order what you will," I tell him, making a grand seigniorial gesture.

"A glass of beer and a plate of pickles—with your permission."

"Landlord, a schooner of beer and a plate of pickles!"

Pete puts on his most beguiling manner, but the Pole does not respond; he arouses my curiosity. Pete sours and begins to fret.

"Will you tell us about yourself?" I include Doyle pronominally but keep my eyes on the stranger, wishing to make my inamorato suffer. "What is your name, friend?"

"Stanisław Herbert, from Gdańsk—*Poland*, mind, not Russia."

"I'm Walt Whitman." It's unlikely he has heard of me; nevertheless, I hope for a sign of recognition from a man who has read all the Bard's tragedies in Polish and in English. Walt, you are a vain old dog!

He shakes my hand; his grip is manly.

Pete remains sullen. "My friend Peter Doyle," I say on his behalf.

Stanisław extends his hand, but Pete keeps his

churlishly pocketed. I'm becoming furious with him. Stanisław takes back his hand and selects a pickle from the plate. Nervously, I wait to see if he will do something rude with it. He puts the pickle in his mouth and chews without ado. The crisp sound of its maceration strips the moment of possibility. It is exquisite, that moment; in it, desire ripens to the threshold of consummation. How often I have watched the apple ripen, tremble, and fall—exulting in the trembling, regretting the fall! But tonight, the pickle is nothing but a pickle.

Apples, pickles—you're making a chutney of this metaphor, Whitman!

Doyle gets up of a sudden and, without a word, leaves the barroom. Outside, he bangs on the window with his fist and calls, "Bring out your dead!"

"Your friend is resentful with me."

"He's not himself tonight. He's usually chirt enough." I'm protective of my sweethearts, even when they disappoint me. But I wonder if tonight he has not gone too far.

"I am sorry."

"How did you come to speak and read English?"

"My father was a merchant in Gdańsk. I lived in a fine house. I had an English tutor. He loved the Immortal Bard. When Father's business was ruined, he hanged himself, and I went on the sea. My brother has written to me that students have uprisen in Poland and Lithuania against the tsar. I go home to be with my brother against the Imperial Russian Army and the Cossacks, who have stolen our country."

Always the convulsion, and the peaceful days are broken, and the Earth itself groans. Men are seized, as by an epileptic fit, and forget themselves. Innocence is derided; tender feelings are scorned. They want what others have, and having it, want more. Their thirst is unslakable; their hunger cannot be appeased. They conquer land, territories, nations entire. A neighbor's farm, orchard, his very dooryard—these, too, they grab. What they covet, they take. The owners of shops and small concerns are swindled out of them by the town's leading citizens, just as sovereign nations are annexed by armies of liberation. Their thirst is intense; it drives them mad, as shipwrecked sailors are driven mad by drinking from the ocean. The hunger for property—both movable and unmovable—is ravenous. Because of it, Africans are taken from the Congo in chains, the aborigines are removed from their homelands, the buffalos are annihilated, and the wards of the hospitals are filled with children. The fit is on again, Oh, world! Emperors, kings, tsars, profiteers, swindlers, shysters, spoilsmen, and assassins, I admonish you—I bid you take heed!

The Pole asks to hear my history. In that my birth at West Hills, not far from Long Island Sound, and my early years there and in Brooklyn were neither more nor less miraculous than any other child's, I omit them from my account. I do make an exception of the glorious Independence Day when I was six and Lafayette kissed me.

"*Vive la France!*" shouts my egalitarian auditor, disturbing the slumbers of a blue jacket whose head is resting on his arm. And then in his language and in mine, he proposes an ecstatic toast to liberty: "*Niech żyje Polska! Niech żyje wolność!* Long live Poland! Long live freedom!" The word final, superior to all.

"To Poland!" I reply, raising my glass of beer. "And to the States and territories!"

Wiping foam from my mustache, I sketch my life's story as it has thus far been revealed to me: I was the second-born of what would be seven brothers and sisters. Having left school at the age of eleven, I worked as a dogsbody in the law office of James B. Clarke and Son on lower Fulton Street in Brooklyn. On some days, I delivered papers to Aaron Burr, who would reward me with a piece of fruit, as if crossing Brooklyn ferry were not treat enough for a boy! Once I saw Andrew Jackson wearing a white beaver hat and Jacob Astor dressed in a mulberry evening coat. God love the one and damn the other to a rich man's hell! Not quite so infernal was a printer's apprenticeship at the Long Island *Patriot,* where the inky words of other men made an impression on the palms of my hand.

The following summer, I mucked about at Worthington's printing house. Later on, I learned to compose type for the *Long-Island Star.* Compositor is an agreeable trade—nay, a necessary one for poets.

How better to appreciate the weight of words than to build them by hand from the cast-metal letters of the alphabet? A word is the poem of poems! How marvelous it is to hold it! To be transfixed by the barbs of its typography!

In 1835, I set type for a Manhattan concern until the Great Conflagration gutted seventeen city blocks and seven hundred buildings, including the custom house, the Merchants' Exchange (the bronze of Alexander Hamilton melted!), and Printing House Square. Burning turpentine set the Hudson aflame. Out of work and funds, I got myself up as an itinerant teacher on Long Island—in East Norwich, Hempstead, Long Swamp, Smithtown, and Babylon. Growing sick of pickled hog's head and cabbage and of sleeping in my pupils' barns in lieu of a salary, I went to work in the pressroom of the *Long-Islander*, at Huntington, and then—a pilgrim making scant progress—in Jamaica, for the *Long Island Democrat*. In 1840, I stumped for Van Buren, who detested the abolitionists, fearing they would break the Union in two. He lost to the Tippecanoe and Tyler Too ticket, scuttling my hopes for patronage. My pockets empty, I was obliged to resume the dispiriting life of the peripatetic schoolmaster.

The following year, I set type for *The New World*. Thereafter, I was employed by the *Aurora*, the *Evening Tattler*, the *Statesman*, the *Plebian*, the New York *Sun*, the *New-York Mirror*, the *Brooklyn Evening Star*, the *Brooklyn Daily Eagle,* and—for a glorious, if brief, season—the *Daily Crescent* of New Orleans, where I sauntered, like any boulevardier, amid fragrant magnolia and dark Creole beauties. I was let go not for idleness but for my Northern sympathies. Returning to New York, I became owner and editor in chief of my own Free Soil paper, the Brooklyn *Weekly Freeman.* The first issue was no sooner printed than the premises burned to the ground. New York was an incendiary town in those days.

I pass over the ensuing five years of low spirits, to a red-letter day in May 1855, when I took out a copyright for the first edition of *Leaves of Grass.* (I say not a word about *Franklin Evans; or, The Inebriate,* a novel I dashed off in three days for seventy-five dollars cash, at Tammany Hall and at the Pewter Mug, soused with port, gin, and whiskey. Nor do I mention my articles in the *Aurora* that rattled paper sabers for Polk, the Mexican War, temperance, and the Democratic Party and incited nativist hooligans to riot. I keep mum, as well, about having defamed the Catholics and the Irish. That I was maligned as a "pretty pup," "dirty fellow," "vagabond," and an "indolent, incompetent loafer," I leave to my biographers to disclose.)

"You have done many things," says the Pole. "I wonder will I."

"Many things but none worth mentioning, except this." I take the copy of *L. of G.* from my coat pocket that I had brought for Doyle—the 1855 edition. I give the book to Stanisław; it will be more appreciated by this foreigner, whom I have known for an hour, than by the horsecar conductor, who, in his carelessness, has lost other of my presents, though he professes to love me.

"You are very kind," says Stanisław. "Please to read something."

He hands me back the book. I open it and recite:

> The Dutchman voyages home, and the
>   Scotchman and Welshman voyage
>   home . . and the native of the
>   Mediterranean voyages home;
> To every port of England, France,
>   Spain, enter wellfilled ships;
> The Swiss foots it toward his hills . . . .
>   the Prussian goes his way, the
>   Hungarian his way, and the Pole
>   goes his way

"You wrote it for me."

"I knew you would come along one day."

He puts on his sailor's cap. "Now I must go to my ship."

We get up from the table. Our chairs scrape against the floor in concert. The man with his head on his arm does not waken. I offer to walk Stanisław to the ship. I put a few coins on the table for the barkeep. I leave a two-cent piece for the sleeper. I put on my coat and soft hat. I cock it on my head, as I please. With my book under his arm, Stanisław goes out into the night air. I follow, shy, as though I were the young man and he the old one. How many nights did I leave Pfaff's beer cellar, underneath the Broadway pavement near Bleecker Street, arm in arm with a lusty young fellow?

The Pole and I walk along the Anacostia to the wharves. The masts of ships are swaying, each in its own way, each one independent of the rest, according to the contrary motions of the water. Taken together, they become a symbol of democracy. I nearly point it out to Stanisław, but he has no experience of freedom and may not grasp the analogy.

He stops at the *Elise Schmidt,* a German bark out of the port of Hamburg. A watchman calls to Stanisław in Polish, and he replies in kind.

"She's a fine ship," I say, although my knowledge of vessels extends only to ferryboats and steam packets, such as I took up the Mississippi and across the Great Lakes on my return to New York from New Orleans.

"She will take me home in good time."

I kiss him as a father would a son leaving for war—as Priam did Hector, whom Achilles would slay on the Plains of Troy. Stanisław smiles. He lifts his cap in friendly salute and walks up the gangway. On deck, he waves my *Leaves* in farewell. I cannot think of a better valediction.

I walk back the way I came. A mist has appeared on the river. When I turn around in the hope of a last look at Stanisław, the ship has vanished.

"WALTER."

I look over my shoulder. For a moment, I think that it is Stanisław who whispered my name, and my heart beats loudly in my chest.

"Walt!" No, it is not the voice of my Polish comrade.

"Who's there?" I ask, more curious than afraid.

A black shape steps into the light cast on the paving by the barroom's lamps. Inside, the barkeep is wiping the tables. The sailor is gone from his place by the window. The two-penny coin I had left for him lies on the table.

"Doyle," I say to the man illumined by the pale light from the window. He seems to be leaning, as if the night were tangible and a man might rest his shoulder against it.

"It's me, Walter."

"What do you want?" I don't feel generous toward him. His near presence excites me, but I have not forgotten his surliness.

"Forgive me." His voice is shy. He has a hang-dog look, which I despise, although his contrition appears genuine. I smile at his confusion. Seconds pass, each one a stone. I think of old Giles Corey on his back as the Puritans piled stone on stone until his chest cracked. Their instruments of torture were more homely than those of Catholic Spain, but we are a resourceful people—we make do with the materials at hand. (How strange to think of friend Hawthorne's great-great-grandfather handing down death warrants from the Salem bench!)

Peter steps backward into the darkness to cower there. I grow alarmed; one can wait too long to forgive, to show magnanimity. A person can have a change of heart—in a moment, he can change from complaisance to resentment; humility can turn rancorous in an instant. I have seen it happen before. In an instant, all can be lost.

"Peter!" I murmur in a honeyed tone; "Pete the Great," as he likes me to call him.

He comes toward me, and we embrace. He kisses me on the lips. "I'm sorry," he says, and he is in earnest. I stroke his unkempt hair. I press him to me and feel the flask of gin in his waistcoat. I smell licorice on his breath, which he chews to hide his drinking. I don't reproach him. If he is, as he fears, a venerealee, I will say nothing against him. Sure of my affection, he begins to behave like a wounded sweetheart. His coquettishness puts me off. I don't care for the languid, mincing tribe or the gray-faced onanists. I despise she-harlots and he-harlots, equally. "The Greek youth became enamored of the *ephebe* in the

gymnasium, where he appeared nude and beautiful."
That line by Alcaeus expresses the ideal.

"Let's go to my room," says Pete.

I may have lost my appetite, but I agree. One eats
too many sweets, swears to give them up, then craves
them. We move forward, and just as readily we with-
draw, only to advance again. Oceanic tides are felt by
men and women alike. Captive, we are in the round
dance of the stars. Arm in arm, Pete and I saunter
to his rooming house on East Nineteenth Street. He
unlocks the door to a second-story room overlooking the poorhouse and the powder magazine. I throw
open the window. The odors of men do not offend
me, who daily breathes them in rank concentrations
in the hospital wards, but I prefer to sleep in the cold
night air. Unencumbered, we lie on the bed without
lighting a candle.

> The married couple sleep calmly in their
>   bed, he with his palm on the hip of
>   the wife, and she with her palm on
>   the hip of the husband,
> The sisters sleep lovingly side by side in
>   their bed,
> The men sleep lovingly side by side in
>   theirs

Darkness covers us. To be two persons together
in it is to know what hands, and hands alone, can
read. Mine are the hands of the compositor setting

letters of type on the composing stick. I have only to feel them to discover their identity. My hands are those of a blind merchant doing sums on an abacus or a connoisseur of objets d'art, following contours of bronze or jade with closed eyes. (The bodies of men and women are the finest objets d'art, and the sum of their qualities defies mathematics!) In darkness, we apprehend essence. Peter and I are in the primal condition. Limitless space and time are pouring through the open window. Were I to shut it, they would continue, undiminished by the dirty panes and undivided by the glazing bars of the sash. Eternity is in Pete Doyle's shabby room as much as it is in royal apartments.

I stand at the window with a blanket covering me. Pete comes and stands beside me. I cover us both with the blanket. I breathe in his rank masculinity.

"What star is that?" he asks, pointing to a green light above the Maryland hills. He is often curious about the stars, and I take it as a sign of his character. If there is good in you, my friend, it lies in your capacity to be awed by the incandescent spheres revolving in tranquillity far beyond our ceaseless perturbations.

"Not a star at all—it's Mercury, named for the messenger of the gods. I doubt it has any words for us." Our ears are stuffed with the blab of hucksters.

"That don't sound like you, Walt! I thought every goddamn blade of grass and bump on the skull has something to say."

I wave my hand as though to shoo a fly. "*Trist-esse*, dear fellow—the gloom that follows satiety." Just the same, I wonder if something else is in the room with us, which has put its arms around me with sinister intention.

Can it be the wards, after all, and the horrors to which I daily devote myself with strange urgency that affect me? One month, and I'm growing chilled like Earth entering a penumbra. Not even a month. How many more months till peace comes round again? How many more hospital visits must I make until then? How many cots filled with young men will I find empty on my return the following day? How many empty sleeves and trouser legs? The sight of a powder magazine and a poorhouse—dead black hulks in the moonless sky—is enough to quench the native optimism.

I was a fat-cheeked apprentice when I stood on the pavement and watched the Leonid meteor shower dazzle the November nights in 1833. I took it as a harbinger of a fortunate life. I may have been mistaken. Sorrow may be my portion after all.

"Why, Walt, you're trembling!"

"What else would I be doing standing naked at the open window?" But it is not the cold that makes me tremble, nor is it the proximity of my darling boy.

Lovingly, Pete presses against me. His warmth is reassuring. "Are you ever afraid?" he asks softly.

"Never!" I say emphatically, aware that I am lying.

THE NEGRO MENIAL SHOVELS CLINKERS into the stove. The rattle of coal pleases me. I put down my pen, crack my knuckles luxuriously, and lean back in my chair to enjoy the view of the distant river. Seen from the upper-story window of the paymaster's building, the boats resemble Jesus bugs striding over the water. I watch the packets, steamers, barges, frigates, gunboats, and corvettes stitch the river with the white threads of their wakes. The pavements are jammed with office seekers, pettifoggers, confidence men, hotheads, and cool customers, each pushing his own interests, each one looking for the main chance. Tradesmen's wagons, flies, horsecars, hansom cabs, and gigs are wheeling through the streets of Georgetown—no two in tandem as each driver pursues his own end.

I put a pot on the sheet-iron stove to make tea. In the agitation of the water as it begins to boil, I recall the signal horror of my youth—the June day in 1829 when the steam frigate *Fulton* exploded in the Brooklyn Navy Yard. In my chest, I felt the immense concussion. (Even now I feel it!) The blast was of sufficient force to catapult four masts fifty feet into the air, destroy the forward decks, and kill thirty officers and crewmen, along with some female visitors to the ship. I was there when they carried the dead ashore, many burned and mangled. I was there—a boy of ten—when the funeral procession arrived at the Fulton Street burying ground. Sailors marched two by two—hand in hand—their banners tied up and bound in black crepe. A squad of soldiers fired rifles over the fresh-made graves.

Stirred by remembrance, I invite the negro to share my lunch. Without a word, he takes the chair opposite mine as I slice a baker's loaf in two and unwrap a lump of butter done up in brown paper.

"Help yourself."

He does, taking the smaller piece of bread and none of the butter. Who can say whether he does so because of a delicate sense of modesty or fear and a habit of submission? Perhaps he doesn't care for butter. Transactions with the colored race are always complicated.

I pour two cups of tea. After I have sweetened mine with sugar scooped from a paper sack, I indicate, with a nod, that he should do the same. He refuses my sugar, curtly. He is not a dim-descended, black, divine-soul'd African, large, fine-headed, nobly-form'd, superbly destin'd, on equal terms with me! He is not ideal, nor is he my equal. His posture suggests a swag of chain; his wool pate appears singed, as though grazed by lightning. Nothing noble or divine sits before me, holding a tin cup in both hands. (How gnarled the fingers, how knobbed! And the skin beneath the nails—how very odd that it should be pink!) Nothing superb awaits him, no destiny, except the indifferent one common to us all. I'm curious to know whence he came. How does one ask a black man to tell his history? Were you a slave? Were you made to wear the slave collar or the iron bit? Did your master sell your wife and children? Is your back sown with scars? How did you get to Washington, how escape your chains? Did you travel by the Underground Railroad? Except for slave narratives written by Frederick Douglass, Samuel Long, James Curry, Solomon Northup, and others published in *The Liberator*, I know almost nothing of negroes and their pains. I've spoken to them on the streets and horsecars and on the docks, coming in and out of the holds of ships bearing great burdens on their backs—but how does one ask a black man to tell his history without giving offense?

At a loss, I say, "Of every hue and caste am I, of every rank and religion." Even to my ears, the *pronunciamiento* sounds pompous. I feel the flush of embarrassment spread across my face and prepare to return the negro's contemptuous glance with one of my own.

There is an amplitude of meanings in his expression, but none I can decipher.

"Have you a name?" My voice is unsteady, and I resent him because of it.

"My master named me after himself. I don't care for it."

"What name do you go by? You must be called

something." Is it Washington, Jefferson, Garrison, or Tennyson? I often encounter the like in the paymaster's books.

"Boy, coon, darky, nigger."

His insolence infuriates me. "You appear to have taken a dislike to me."

"I took nothing, except a piece of bread and a mug of tea."

"I don't begrudge you a little food and drink."

"But you expect me to perform for them!" he retorts, dismissing my largesse. "You're no different from the lady who used to give me a piece of pie for a Bible verse or a 'coon song.' She was a good Christian, too."

"I don't claim to be a good Christian!" I reply, growing warm.

"I supposed you was, seeing how you work for the Christian Commission."

"I *volunteer* in the wards. The treats I buy for the soldiers are all on my own hook."

"That gives us something in common, Mr. Whitman: I used to volunteer in the tobacco fields, and more than once I got hung up on a hook."

"I dress black men's wounds, the same as I do those of white men!"

"Were you surprised the first time you saw that a black man's blood was red?"

"I don't think we have anything to say to each other."

"I don't suppose we do."

"Then I wish you a good day."

He takes his coal scuttle and goes, leaving me furious.

I PUSH A WOUNDED SOLDIER sitting in a bath chair across Armory Square Mall to Ward D to see his brother, who arrived this morning on a train from Maryland. He has been put among the "veal," as new casualties are called. On the chill mall, dispirited cattle graze the splintery grass. An army recruit arrives, wheeling a barrow. He forks hay into a manger. Aroused by the sweet smell, the cattle go to the trough and begin to eat. The young man—he looks to me no older than fifteen or sixteen—raises the fork. For an instant before he jabs it into the ground, his eyes are dazzled by sunlight glimmering on the tines. He pats the rumps of the animals affectionately. Because it is winter, no flies torment them (and in the wards, no maggots moil in the men's wounds). The boy pulls his fork from the frozen earth. He lifts his head to regard the President's House. He tugs an ear and looks toward the balcony where Mr. Lincoln sometimes paces. Perhaps he is wondering if the "Rail Splitter" is up to the job. Many believe that he is not, as—by battle and skirmish—the Union pays dearly for his principles.

The president is disheartened by his generals.

Each seems to lack the will to engage with the enemy. Winfield Scott, who served in the War of 1812 and the Mexican-American War, has grown too fat to mount his horse. McClellan built a crackerjack army, but he was either too cautious or too nervous to use it, regardless of how Lincoln cajoled, implored, and threatened him. After the Union calamities on the Virginia Peninsula, the president replaced "Little Mac," as his men called him, with "Old Brains" Henry Halleck, senior commander of our western forces. Although an able strategist, he, too, has been reluctant to commit his troops against Lee's. I heard from a staff officer down with malaria in the sick ward that Mr. Lincoln said of him that he was "little more than a first-rate clerk."

On the mall, the young man strokes the flanks of the cattle, shoulders his fork, and walks toward the white tents pitched on the grass. With tens of thousands of soldiers in Washington, tents crowd every park and greensward. Men billet in houses, hotels, government buildings—even the Capitol, in the basement of which masons built twenty brick ovens to bake soldiers' bread. Congressmen complain that they cannot do the people's business without tripping over invalids. I think their business must be going at full bore—the people's representatives look so fat and prosperous.

My wounded soldier asks me to stop. In an earlier life, he and his brother worked their family farm in New Hampshire, on the Gale River in Franconia. "They're keeping them alive so's they can slaughter them in the spring," he says of the cattle, which have walked on to drink at a muddy brook that runs into the noxious canal.

He does not draw the obvious comparison, nor do I draw it for him.

"I heard there are ten thousand beeves on the hoof in Washington City," he says.

"And a parcel of jackasses dressed in striped pants."

Everywhere, one hears talk of a siege. When every last stalk of hay and blade of grass is grazed and the livestock, down to the last chicken scratching in the dooryard, has been butchered, how long before the city is starved into submission? Lee and his generals will cut off the nation's head. I once shared a seat in a railway car with a drummer in farm implements who claimed to have seen a chicken in Peekskill live two weeks without its head. "I don't believe it," I replied. "Can you believe a week?" he asked. If the capital gets lopped off, the body politic will wobble in the door- yard awhile before the heart of the Leviathan stops. God help the negroes then!

"We kept Red Angus for milk and meat and an ox for plowing," says the chairbound soldier wistfully. I suppose in his mind's eye he is seeing the homestead, his mother and sisters perched on milking stools, his brother and father in the field, the father walking behind the plow, his young son walking beside the ox and shooing the flies from its back with a hazel switch. I picture the share cutting the delicious chocolate earth and the blackbirds wading stiff-legged in the fresh furrows as they tug up worms.

I wheel the soldier into the ward and down the main aisle separating the rows of cots. Armory Square Hospital has room for a thousand men inside its twelve pavilions. The sick and wounded come and go, but the cots are always filled. Nearby the far wall, the soldier finds his brother, who, as it happens, is missing his right leg. The man I have been pushing is missing his left one. The grim coincidence sparks a volley of comical patter some might consider morbid. I do not regard it as such. It's a brave show, and the two brothers are superb.

"The carpenter's making me a hollow wooden leg that'll hold a quart of bark juice."

"Boys of the Fourth Illinois used to play baseball with Santa Anna's wooden leg. They'd jayhawked it while he was eating his lunch. He didn't miss it till he'd finished his tamales—they were that slick! After the war, some bluffers took it round the county fairs. Cost a dime to see it—two bits for a feel of it."

"Not many rubes'll plunk down a quarter of a dollar to have a feel of *your* wooden leg!"

"As I recall, yours ain't any great shakes, either, my darling timber toe."

"I knew a fella got his johnson shot off."

"No more logrolling for that boyo."

"Why, I'd rather lose both legs than my holy poker!"

"I say, better to have lost a leg than a hand."

"Certainly! You need two to play cards."

"Three would be better."

"An extra sleeve *would* come in handy."

"Let's put on a big coat and pass ourselves off as a two-headed man."

"If one of us blacks up—why hell, the suckers'll shit goobers!"

"We'll be the talk of the lyceums and the Sunday schools."

"A walking illustration of the dangers of amalgamating the races."

"The Racial Anomaly."

"We'll hire ourselves out to Barnum."

I hear the impudent words of the soldiers. I witness their audacity before God. I stand amazed and admiring. Such men as these the prophet Joel enjoined, "Beat your plowshares into swords, and your pruning hooks into spears: let the weak say, I am strong." These two brothers answered the martial call. They put away the old life as a thing unworthy. They left the peaceful homestead behind them; they left tranquillity behind them. They took up rifles and bayonets and made war against the enemies of union. I will leave all and come and make the hymns of you.

I think about John Brown, who was hanged

for insurrection. Lieutenant Colonel Robert E. Lee was in Charles Town, coolly giving his orders to the hanging party. Lieutenant J. E. B. Stuart was with Lee, serving as his aide-de-camp; it was he whom Lee had sent to parley with "Old" Brown and his acolytes inside the U.S. arsenal's engine house at Harper's Ferry. Lee and Jeb Stuart were for the States then. Fort Sumter had yet to be fired on. Jeff Davis was a United States senator. I was in the engine house with Brown. Later, I was at the place of his execution. I watched the old man, tall, with white hair, mount the scaffold in Virginia. Meteor of the war! I mounted the sky with him who was assumed into heaven. Being mortal, I went only a little way with him.

I think about the seven thousand Greeks at Thermopylae, who defied Xerxes' army of a million men. I recall the Maccabees, who refused to renounce their faith, and the Jews of Masada, who chose self-slaughter rather than an ignoble death or a humiliating enslavement by Rome. I remember the Bohemian reformer Jan Hus, disciple of Wycliffe, whom the Italian prelates sent to the stake. Joan of Arc, whom the English burned for heresy, she, too, I remember, as well as the Protestant Waldensians massacred by the Catholic duke of Savoy, of whom Milton wrote, "Slain by the bloody Piemontese that rolled / Mother with infant down the rocks."

I remember Milton's adjuration of God in his eighteenth sonnet: ". . . in thy book, record their groans"—the groans of the Waldensians and of all who love liberty and suffer at the hands of tyrants. I will write such a book—a memorandum of incidents, persons, places, sights. I will keep the accounts and do the sums: one dead man added to another, while another waits to be added and, soon enough, is added to the numbing record. How soon the page is filled with names of men and boys as the columns increase! How quickly the gray ledgers fill with Union dead and, also, with that of the Confederacy (not forgetting that the men and boys whose coats are oatmeal gray were born in American latitudes). One, two, buckle my shoe; three, four, shut the door.

"It's only a matter of arithmetic," I tell the brothers, who are looking at me strangely. "A schoolboy could do as well."

I put my hand over my heart and sing till my voice, always so lusty, cracks:

> Gory, gory, Hallelujah!
> Gory, gory, Hallelujah!
> Gory, gory, Hallelujah!
> His truth is marching on.

I feel faint. I hear hornets sizzle past my ears. My head begins to spin; I see black, and my eyes sting, as happens sometimes when one comes out of strong sunlight into darkness. I ask the brothers their pardon. I turn away from the reunion. I mumble a few words and leave them to stare after me. I go outside and pass among the grim clusters precisely arranged on the mall. The cattle take fright at the sight of a wild man whose gray beard is flying in his confusion. I croak a verse from Jeremiah. I stop a moment and am sick in the splintery grass.

"You've breathed too much effluvia," says a surgeon. Finishing his auscultation, he puts away his stethoscope. "You oughtn't to make so many visits to the wards. Illness spreads from man to man through the noxious atmosphere. Infections and fevers jump like fleas from bed to bed. Rest in your own bed, Mr. Whitman, before you end up sick to death in one of these." He lifts his hand to take in the rows of cots, then lets it drop, as if his hand has absorbed all of the ward's weariness and despondency. "You're liable to be sent home a 'lunger,' if you don't take care."

I LIE IN BED, ENJOYING THE TEARS I have coaxed from my eyes. Sorrow can be sweet, like the taste of a rotted tooth. I think of the two brothers. I forgive them their affronted look; my parting words—which, muttered in delirium, I cannot recall—incensed them. It is wonderful to forgive, luxurious to grant pardon; this the stiff-necked judges and sanctimonious churchmen who delight in our damnation do not comprehend. Nevertheless, I don't fall immediately to sleep, as is habitual for me, whose conscience is clean as his bowels. Perhaps you need a purge,

Walt—a dose of salts to ease your mind of the hard stool of thought. Gloom invades the small bedroom. It puts its hand on my arm like a drunkard who wants me to join him in the remorse that follows dissipation. I get dressed and quietly leave the house.

Once again I find myself at Armory Square. I seem drawn to the place as I used to be drawn to ride the Brooklyn ferry. The gaslights are turned low. Most of the men are sleeping, except for those kept sleepless by pain. Several nurses are passing amid the cots. Now and again, one calls to a surgeon. The voice is calm, despite the urgency of the occasion. Night comes in at the windows. It billows like black smoke underneath the ceiling; it lies thickly on the rafters like a black moss; it hides underneath the cots; it drapes the cots funereally.

"Evening, Walt," says one of the attendants, who is not surprised by my visit, although the night is advanced.

"Evening, Charles," I reply, much at ease. "All well?"

"Except for the poor fella shot through the bladder. He died an hour ago."

Died while I was fitfully tossing in my bed in an ecstasy of emotion. I take off my hat, as if his corpse were nearby, but they have removed the body to make room for a cavalry officer shot through the spleen.

I wish Charles a good night and go to the back of the ward, where the brother missing his right leg has his cot. I find him asleep and pull up a chair to keep him company. I sit for a while, quietly watching his chest rise and fall. I think that if his lungs were to cease in their respiration, I'd go mad. They would give me the corset to wear and pack me off to the Government Hospital for the Insane, with a recommendation from Nurse Dix that I be kept there for the war's duration. Would Peter Doyle visit, I wonder, and would he bring me little treats? I doubt O'Connor would—not after our row—but his wife might. Lately, I have sensed a nervousness in her; she is like a bird held in one's hand, its small heart beating fast. I think, perhaps, she is infatuated with me. In the darkness behind my closed eyes, I see how the bodies of men and women engirth me.

I open my eyes to the murkiness. The amputee has not awakened, nor has he died. The world is balanced on a razor's edge. My gaze wanders over the slumbering bodies, supine or prostrate, and comes to rest on the figure of a man standing in the middle of the ward. He leans over someone who has been softly groaning, so as not to disturb his comrades. The visitor is a tall, thin man, his face—what I can see of it in the light of the lamp he holds—is creased and gaunt. His narrow shoulders are covered by a shawl. When he stands, his figure casts a lengthy shadow. Have you also come to keep watch, O my Captain? I've heard that you sometimes walk the half mile from the President's House to Armory Square to pass amid the casualties and clasp their hands firmly in yours, although tonight is the first time I have seen you here. I saw you last two years ago, when you stood in front of the Astor House and gazed imperturbably on a sullen mob of thirty thousand. You had few admirers among them, and fewer friends. I half-expected the Copperheads to leap at you en masse and tear you limb from limb. You looked at me, and I at you, and I knew that fate had shackled us.

I remember Mathew Brady's likeness of presidential candidate Lincoln, displayed at the Daguerrean Miniature Gallery on Broadway. He was clean-shaven, but even then the hollow cheeks and mournful eyes were conspicuous in the unprepossessing face. He had come to New York's Cooper Union to argue that nothing in the Constitution forbids the federal authority from prohibiting slavery in the territories. I was there, and saw what Brady saw through his camera lens—the steel of the man, the look in his eyes, which might be sadness or an anger too large for so spare a frame. The face was lined, though not so deeply as the furrows I see there now, drawn by care and revealed by the stark shadows thrown by the lamp. At Brady's gallery, I studied the younger facsimile of the face before me, but I never could understand the expression, laid down by light on grains of silver, in Abe Lincoln's eyes.

I would go and shake his hand, but something forbids it—nothing in him, for he is the least forbidding of men, but in me. I doubt he is aware of me in this dark corner where I sit and watch him pass slowly from bed to bed, stopping a moment at each one to bow his head. I cannot tell whether it is in prayer or in pity that he does. I would go to him and put my arms around him; I would tell him that, at the outset, I misjudged his strength and goodness. But I remain where I am, acknowledging the gulf between us, which I will never cross, except in death.

Mr. Lincoln leaves the ward, and tears come to my eyes for a second time that night. Is there nothing so pathetic as an old man's tears? I follow him, assured that, if he should turn his head, he could not see me in the darkness. We walk together in silence. He does not know that a frightened man is trailing after him. He climbs into a carriage and sits beside an army officer. I see the "pumpkin rinds" on his shoulders, but I am not near enough to tell his rank. He fans the horses, and the carriage starts off. I am surprised when it does not stop at the President's House but continues in the direction of the river and the basin. I have heard that Lincoln will visit the Old Naval Observatory of an evening to console himself with the vast vaults of eternity. I don't know if he seeks the Almighty there or wishes simply to lose himself among the remotest stars. To be put in his place sometimes does a man good. To feel small in the presence of the sublime, whether the firmament, the oceans, or the Himalayas, can be a comfort. For a moment, one need not worry about his wardrobe, his wallet, his politics, or his courage. To put on airs before such immensity is ridiculous. Better that humbling than the vanity of a big fish in a small pond, which is dangerous: A careless motion of its tail can scuttle ships and swamp Earth's high places.

I go back to my room in L Street. The house is quiet. In the two rooms above mine, the O'Connors have gone chastely to bed. Since little Philip died of smallpox, the marriage bed has been cold. William is too handsome for plain Nelly, who is in mourning. Her shy glances across the supper table disturb me. Does William notice them? I wonder.

I make an entry in my memoranda book, a few small folded and stitched scraps of paper:

> The white portico—the brilliant gas-light shining—the palace-like portico—the tall, round columns, spotless as snow—the walls also—the tender and soft moonlight, flooding the pale marble, and making peculiar faint languishing shades, not shadows—everywhere too a soft transparent haze, a thin blue moonlace, hanging in the night in the air—the brilliant and extra plentiful clusters of gas, on and around the facade, columns, portico, &c.—everything so white, so marbly pure and dazzling, yet soft—the White House of future poems, and of

dreams and dramas, there in the soft and copious moon—the pure and gorgeous front, in the trees, under the night-lights, under the lustrous flooding moon, full of reality, full of illusion—The forms of the trees, leafless, silent, in trunk and myriad-angles of branches, under the stars and sky—the White House of the land, the White House of the night, and of beauty and silence—sentries at the gates, and by the portico, silent, pacing there in blue overcoats—stopping you not at all, but eyeing you with sharp eyes, whichever way you move.

Walt, you are plastering yourself over with poems and memoranda, newspaper accounts and jeremiads, with ledger pages reeking of mortality. Soon you will not recognize yourself. Or have you already lost yourself as surely and cruelly as the amputees their limbs? Which loss, I wonder, is the more terrible? I am the poet of suffering. I am with the sick and the wounded. I give them what comfort I may.

Listen to yourself, old fool! What is your suffering compared to theirs? You must stop this posing. It makes you ridiculous.

What does it matter so long as the poems get written, so long as *Leaves* continue to grow on the sap of circumstances? And don't I cheer and console the boys? Don't I spend myself to the last ounce and cent?

I give them my body to eat and my blood to drink, till one day nothing will be left of Walt Whitman, except his book. Nonetheless, I think that that will be enough for me—enough for any man or woman who is afraid to slip away unnoticed. *Leaves of Grass* shall be my sepulcher—my green plot of earth.

Superb egotist!

WILLIAM O'CONNOR, WHOM I KNEW in Boston before the war, clerks at the Light-House Board, near Lafayette Square. Seldom have I encountered a more passionate talker. He can argue the wings off a fly or a fly off a turd. Like most of his hotheaded race, he is fond of argument and will opine on subjects as various as Shakespeare (he claims Francis Bacon wrote the plays), the Brooklyn Atlantics vis-à-vis the Buffalo Niagaras (he favors the former), the best places to eat beefsteak in the capital, none of which he can afford, or the most picturesque estaminet in Paris, where he has never been and is likely never to go. Generally, I let him dragoon me. His politics, however, will sometimes make me hot. His opinions can lie heavily on the stomach, like a week-old Irish scone. I try to keep shy of controversy till I've finished my supper and we have got on to the port and cigars, which burn like straw and smell like dung. A former mill girl from Lowell, Nelly considers our "terrible combats" trivial. She speaks fire against the exploitation of women and children but has no words to waste on literary provenance, baseball, beefsteaks, or Parisian cafés.

Ah, but you are undesirable, Nelly! And William, slender, handsome, and virile, takes his rough pleasure in other beds than yours.

Last time they had me to supper, he and I "raised snakes," as Pete Doyle calls a ruckus. Alerted by a passerby to a murder under way at 394 L Street North, a policeman pounded on the door. William placated him with a glass of inferior whiskey. He asked for another, then another, and, admonishing us not to disturb his peace again that night, staggered out the door.

"I'm for emancipation," I said, picking up the hot potato of the age, which whiskey had made hotter.

"But are you for the *negro?*" demanded William. So abruptly did he stand that his chair toppled.

"I am."

"And what is your opinion, Whitman, of that maltreated race?" Blue eyes flashing, his napkin hanging underneath his chin like an undone cravat, he grasped the end of the table with both hands, as though to keep himself from flying at my throat.

"My *conviction* is that the war must stop!" The table, which had been laden with plates of pork, parsnips, and beets, had brought to mind a lieutenant of cavalry—abdomen laid open, the gangrenous wound beyond my power to cleanse or the surgeon's to mend.

The young man's piteous groans had been audible above the clash of cutlery, the sawing of meat with a kitchen knife, and the mashing of beets with a fork. Their blood was not redder than his.

William, who has never clawed the convulsing earth to burrow with the moles, bitten a stick in two while trying to muffle his shrieks, or retched at the stench of his own unraveled innards, declared, "This war is Armageddon come at last to crush the overseers and put an end to the terrible iniquity of slavery."

"This particular Armageddon is about nine hundred and ninety-nine parts diarrhea to one part glory." I unfolded the *Daily National Republican* I had brought to the table and cited the number of the dead and wounded for the first week of January. "I don't care for the niggers in comparison with all this suffering and the dismemberment of the Union." I tore the newspaper to pieces in my indignation. "Slavery *is* a crying sin, but it is not the *only* crying sin in the universe."

He yanked off his napkin and threw it in my face. He was once again the boy his friends called "d'Artagnan," the irascible musketeer. "You're a bigot, Walt."

"I exist as I am; that is enough."

His face turned scarlet. "Goddamn you for a Copperhead, Whitman!"

"Goddamn you for a flannel-mouthed zealot, O'Connor!" Since he was waving the meat fork wildly, I stopped short at ridiculing his fatuous novel, *Harrington: A Story of True Love*. Nelly's articles published in *The Liberator* and the suffragists' paper *The Una* are worth a hundred Harringtons.

I left their apartment, slamming the door behind me. (My indignation had an element of affectation in it—to this, I readily confess.) Returning to my small room, I threw myself on the bed and raged against all those who would send men to "Armageddon" wearing cardboard boots and uniforms made of shredded rags and glue. Accompanied by shrill martial anthems played by a fancy Zu Zu band, bloated declamations of local big bugs, benedictions of scrawny churchmen, and patriotic doggerel of poetesses, the poor lambs embark on the great crusade—army rifle shells packed with sawdust and knapsacks stuffed with weeviled biscuits, gangrened beef, a Bible, and a tract provided by the Sanitary Commission on the dangers of dancing. War is no forge on which men's character is hammered into shape; it deforms and misshapes character, as it does the mortal part.

I swear I am no bigot. Does it not say in my *Leaves* that I comforted the runaway slave and invited him into my house? "And brought water and fill'd a tub for his sweated body and bruis'd feet, / And gave him a room that entered from my own, and gave him some coarse clean clothes"? Although it was my persona who showed mercy, he spoke for me, as I speak for what is human—the gall and the sweet. How can it be otherwise for one whose life is comprehensive, who is of the world and contains the world? Or do you delude yourself by thinking that a man or a woman is either all good or all bad? I make appointments with all.

STEELED TO ENTER THE COCKPIT AGAIN, I go upstairs to the O'Connors' rooms. William is your friend, Walt, I remind myself. He considers you the chief poet of the age. You have only to look at the daguerreotype he made of you in New York to be reminded of his devotion.

"Walt!" says William, touching the sleeve of my coat. His eyes are moist with contrition. Behind him, Nelly stands, thin and stiff in her mourning clothes.

"Come in," says William.

"Wipe your big feet!" admonishes Nelly, smiling. Even though she is grieving, she gazes affectionately at me. Old dog, I do believe you've made another conquest!

William takes my hand and draws me through the doorway. In his hand, I feel the galvanic current of goodwill.

I smell bacon and boiled cabbage. Nelly is dealing out the plates and tableware. William has his napkin tucked into his collar. We take our places onstage, in a play that may be comic or tragic. I await the unfolding as I await the denouement, when the truth of all things will be made apparent. Raising the meat fork, William quotes from one of my poems:

> Something I cannot see puts upward
> > libidinous prongs,
> Seas of bright juice suffuse heaven.

"Amen!" I say.

Nelly gives me the largest portion. William appears not to notice my priority. He eats without an appetite. Nelly picks at her cabbage leaves. Afterward, she clears the table, while William brings a bottle of Blue Ruin and a box of cigars. I wait for developments. He doesn't seem inclined to snarl over some bone of contention. The conversation is desultory. I mention the baseball diamond marked out on the lawn of the President's House, hidden by snow and waiting for spring. Mr. Lincoln loves the game; so do the soldiers who wind yarn around a walnut, cover it with horsehide, and carry it in their packs. Nelly goes into the kitchen to wash the supper things. I hear the scraping of plates and the clash of cutlery.

"I see great things in baseball," I say, gazing at the ceiling, as if I could read the future in the tumbling tobacco smoke. "It's the American game."

The conversation backs and fills until it arrives at Fort Hindman, at Arkansas Post. Last week, nine Union gunboats pounded the earthworks raised above the mouth of the Arkansas to frustrate our advance toward Little Rock. Thirty-three thousand infantrymen packed into fifty transports disembarked below Red Bluff to assail the Confederate position. From trenches and rifle pits, the rebels fired on the long blue column until the guns of our ironclads drove them back across the mud flats to the fort. Caught on piles of logs laid down by the rebels, the U.S.S. *Rattler* was torn apart by Confederate shells. Only the tallow-smeared hulls of our remaining gunboats saved them from the enemy's raking fire. We returned it hotly; fierce cannonading broke open Fort Hindman's earthen walls as, one by one, its guns flickered out of action. Five thousand graybacks surrendered to McClernand, who then ordered Fort Hindman burned.

Calmly, we discuss the notorious character of Brigadier General Grant—his triumphs in Western Tennessee, his humiliation at Shiloh, our hopes for his eventual capture of Vicksburg and the expulsion of the Confederate army from the western bank of the Mississippi.

I think that O'Connor must be sick—he is so unlike himself. To see his eyes flash and his complexion ruddy with anger, I express my grave doubts concerning amalgamation. "For their own good, the negroes should be returned to Africa after the war, at the government's expense." Not even this provocation nettles him.

Exasperated, I ask, "Why the long face? Is one of your 'Washington beauties' making life hell?" The thought of Peter Doyle and his venery springs to mind. "You don't have the tokens of Venus buttoned up inside your pantaloons, do you?"

"I take good care not to."

"What is it, then?"

"This morning I showed Mathew Brady an album of my New York daguerreotypes. I offered to photograph the battlefields, like Gardner, Pywell, and O'Sullivan. Here, O'Connor, I said to myself, is a real, honest job for you. I'm fed up to the teeth with clerking! I'm dying to prove my worth. Damned *Harrington*! I can think of nothing more trivial than love stories! By God, I need to pull myself out of this federal swamp and dung heap!"

I can't imagine William hauling a heavy tripod camera though mud and snow. His métier is the parlor; his subjects are well-upholstered men dressed in frock coats and cutaways, their ladies in hooped skirts and bishop's sleeves beside them. He's familiar with the smirk and simper seen in drawing rooms, not the grimace on the faces of the dying and the dead.

"What did Brady think of the idea?" I ask, concealing my skepticism behind a chuff of cigar smoke.

"He admired my images—he called them 'refined.' He wondered, though, if I had any experience with the wet-plate process. He has no use for daguerreotypes. He needs negatives, which can be reproduced. The demand for stereopticon cards showing corpses is voracious."

Curiosity is the great thing, I say to myself. It is the driver of progress and a hallmark of democracy. But I wonder what effect the trade in images will have on the war. Will it excite pity or enmity? Will people North and South alike demand a cessation of hostilities, or retribution?

"He said, he didn't doubt that I could master the technical aspects of the medium. But he wondered if my 'aesthetics'—he called it that—were compatible with the brutish and grotesque."

William paused. I cleared my throat, in lieu of expressing an opinion. William went on.

"He showed me *The Dead of Antietam*, an album of photographs taken by Alexander Gardner. As he turned the pages, I grew numb. Never have I seen sights so ghastly, so repellent in their grim accumulation! To take as one's subject matter men dead and dismembered, their eyes staring in their sockets, bloated, flyblown horses, ruin, waste, filth! Brady was still turning the pages of the damned book when I shut my eyes, appalled. I wanted to be sick on the Turkey carpet. I've seen engravings in the newspapers of Bull Run and Antietam. Surrounded by adverts for homeopathic remedies, horse powder, and corsets, a battlefield has all the interest of a cricket pitch. I felt Brady's eyes on me. I think I blushed like a schoolgirl.

"'Well, Mr. O'Connor?' he said as he closed Gardner's album.

"For once, I was speechless. I was staring at a

paper knife on his desk. The light from the window caught its blade. I couldn't tear my eyes away.

"'Mr. O'Connor, are you all right?'

"I stammered something—I don't know what—picked up *my* album—how frivolous the contents seemed—and hurried out the door. I hadn't the presence of mind to close it behind me. I stood in the street, quite light in the head. Walt, he put me in my place without needing to utter a word of criticism."

"Ladies and gents, even their snotty brats, deserve to be photographed," I tell him without conviction. "Likenesses of the Brooks brothers ought to be saved for posterity." So that posterity can revile them for getting rich by making shabby clothes for slaves and shoddy uniforms for the Union army.

"You don't really believe that, do you, Walt?"

"No, I don't," I frankly reply. By his sharp glance, I doubt William appreciates my honesty.

"You're a great poet; your themes are large. You can't imagine the wretchedness of mediocrity."

"You'd soon get used to the reality of death en masse and its nauseous particulars if you volunteered for the wards," I say, wanting to sting him. "One quickly becomes inured—that is to say, stupefied." (Or one doesn't and takes to the hills or to the bottle.)

"I've been poor company," he says, pouring himself another whiskey.

I bid him a good night. As I lie in my solitary bed, I'm visited by the revulsion that sometimes comes to a man who has filled a room with his own opinions like a bad odor.

"IS IT ANIMAL, VEGETABLE, or mineral?"

The wounded soldier deliberates awhile before replying, "Animal."

"Can you do without it?" I ask.

"Have to."

"Yes or no, Fred."

This afternoon, I'm in Georgetown, playing twenty questions with a corporal of the Third Regiment Massachusetts Volunteers, a pastime for the bedridden, who, when they are not in pain, despair of the endless tedium. Unlike Armory Square's clean and airy pavilions, Union Hospital used to be a seedy hotel patronized by clerks, itinerants, and mice. The tiny windows are hardly adequate to rid the wards of stink and gloom. Sanitary considerations yield to the necessity posed by so many thousands of casualties arriving each week. After one slaughter, I saw wounded men inside Christ Church, laid on planks set across pew backs.

The corporal scratches his bristled chin in thought. I make a note to shave him next time I visit. Finally, he replies, "Yes."

"Is it yours?" I ask.

Once again he takes time to consider. "It was, so I guess it still is."

"Does it have a distinctive odor?"

"A powerful one, I expect."

"Does it go about on four feet?"

"No."

"Two feet?"

"No."

"Does it crawl?"

"Nope. Leastways, I hope not."

"It is animal, unessential, has a smell, neither walks nor crawls, and it belongs to you. Then it isn't a dog, a cat, a snake, or a wife."

"Haven't got a wife."

"Is it edible?"

"Hell no!"

"Is it white?"

"No."

"Is it black?"

"Yes."

"Would I find it in your chamber pot?"

"No!"

"Is it bigger than a chamber pot?"

"Yes."

"Is it bigger than a trunk?"

"It could fit inside a trunk."

"Is it made of wood?"

"Didn't I say it was animal? Walt, I want to change one of my answers. It ain't animal so much anymore as mineral. I guess you'd call it that. I know it ain't vegetable."

"You aren't allowed to change your answers; however, I'll allow it. So it's mineral, fits into a steamer trunk, is black in color, has an odor, belongs to you, and you can do without it."

The corporal nods, beaming; he is clearly enjoying the game. "Give up?"

I shake my head. "It wouldn't be coal, would it?"

"Coal! That's rich! Coal don't smell."

"It does when you burn it."

"Well, it ain't coal!"

"Damnit, Fred!"

Gleefully, he slaps his thigh. I am charmed to see the boy still inside the haggard veteran of the battles of Kinston, White Hall, and Goldsboro Bridge. He was mauled by a Williams gun during the Union assault on the Wilmington and Weldon Railroad near the railroad bridge, meant to relieve the pressure on Burnside's harassed troops at Fredericksburg. It was a bloodbath.

"Is it a baseball bat?"

"Bats are vegetable, and they ain't black, either, lessin they're real bats; then they're all to pieces animal! It's time you cried 'Uncle!'"

I shake my head, trying not to appear annoyed. "I've got three guesses left."

"I bet you a jar of crabapple jelly you won't guess it." For a while, he forgets himself.

"It's the mineral part's got me stumped! If it were animal, black, and malodorous, I'd guess it was your socks, which are so grimy and stiff, they can walk all by themselves."

"Well, it ain't socks! And I'm counting that as a question, which leaves you two."

I am growing fretful. Ordinarily, the boys are no match for my powers of ratiocination, as Poe's M. Dupin would have said. Well, shame on you, Walt Whitman! In your peevishness, you are no better than William O'Connor. "Is it teeth?" I blurt.

"Teeth?" repeats Fred, taken by surprise.

"You were a New Bedford whaleman. I guess you have a whale tooth or a sea lion's tusk shut up in your trunk."

"There ain't no trunk, Walter! The trunk was your idea. And who in hell ever saw a black tusk! Last guess, old man."

"Frankly, I don't care a fart!"

"Say 'Uncle,' then."

"'Nuncle, give me an egg, and I'll give thee two crowns.'"

"I don't know about that, but the answer is my missing leg!"

My gaze falls on the empty place beneath the sheet. This morning, I cleaned and dressed the weeping stump.

"Pretty damn good, don't you think, Walter?"

"You got the best of me this time," I admit.

"I wish I had that leg—the bone, I mean. I could carve scenes of Kinston, where I lost it. Course they burned it after they sawed it off. I used to make the daintiest scrimshaws you ever seen."

How many amputated legs have I carried to the hospital incinerator for burning? They go into the fire without a prayer being said, as if they had never been part of someone who ran ecstatically down the green aisles of summer corn, ice-skated on a farmer's pond, or danced—scarcely able to breathe—with his sweetheart.

Fred lays his head on his pillow and closes his eyes. I hold his hand a moment, and then I drop the mosquito netting over him. Not even in Washington are there gallinippers in winter, but the netting affords the men some privacy. I leave Fred to his thoughts.

I STAND IN THE DOORWAY, waiting for Nurse Wright to finish. Handsome and peart, she became an army nurse before Dorothea Dix ruled that only plain women over thirty may tend the casualties. Sex is urgent, the impulse to copulate irresistible, but I don't believe that it raises its angry head from the body's ruins. Glancing at the other side of the cheerless ward, I notice the dark-haired woman I saw here once before. She is efficiently shaving a man in a wheelchair.

Having finished the day's tasks, Nurse Wright

accompanies me outside into M Street and the biting cold.

"Shall we get some 'rio' to warm ourselves?" I ask, stuffing my hands into my pockets.

"Let's do!" she replies as she winds her muffler around her throat.

From a coffeehouse near the basin, I see the tents of the First Regiment of U.S. Colored Troops stationed on Mason's Island. Many in Washington believe that the negroes will run if "Old Jack's" boys come thundering across Long Bridge or the aqueduct connecting the capital and Virginia. Although the enemy is, for the moment, a hundred miles northwest of the Potomac, the city remembers in its nerves the shameful rout at First Bull Run, as well as the August day in 1814 when the British burned the President's House, the unfinished Capitol, the Treasury, and the Supreme Court Building. War is mercurial, and Washingtonians may awake one morning to the rebel yell.

On Mason's Island, a company of infantrymen is practicing; I hear rifle fire in the distance.

"Do you feel ill at ease, Miss Wright?" I ask after we have settled ourselves.

"Among the wounded?"

"No, I've seen your compassion for the boys. You're a good nurse, Harriet, and a fine young woman."

She blushes charmingly.

"What I meant to say was, do you feel vulnerable to an attack on the city?"

"Not with so many thousands of our soldiers about, and so many forts and batteries. I can't believe Robert E. Lee and Jefferson Davis would be foolish enough to assail us in our own stronghold."

"In my experience, fools do the most harm in war, as well as in peace."

"Well, I don't suppose General Jackson will surprise us at our coffee and biscuits. Not with a battery of soldiers on Mason's Island."

Among Stonewall Jackson's nicknames is "Tom Fool."

"Last week, I went to the island with Major Hapgood to pay the colored troops. Jackson's boys would roll right over them."

Washington is a tick waiting to be plucked and burned. It may be garrisoned with 23,000 soldiers and defended by sixty forts, ninety-three batteries, 837 guns, and twenty miles of rifle trenches, but I don't underestimate the strength of the Confederacy or the resolve of desperate men. The rebels have yet to be cornered. God help us if they are; they'll leap at our vitals like famished rats.

I spread jam on a biscuit and continue. "Half of Georgetown is secesh and would be overjoyed to see the Confederate army take the District and, by doing so, decapitate the Union."

"Are you trying to scare me, Mr. Whitman?"

"You don't strike me as a person liable to take fright. No, I'm curious about our female nurses—their characters, virtues, qualities, and, in particular, their courage. And I see no harm or impropriety if you were to call me by my Christian name. I give you my word, I am no Caliban."

She smiles once again.

Harriet, you are a charmer!

"Nobody I know is scared to be in Washington, though we sometimes are of losing the war."

"You don't believe that the Union can be beaten by a pack of pie eaters, butternuts, and goober grabbers, do you, Harriet?"

"They're not easily beaten, it seems to me."

The sudden earnestness in her face makes me want to taunt her. "You're not secesh, are you, Nurse Wright? You're not secretly in favor of secession?"

"No! I'm for the Union and the colored people! My mother belongs to the Philadelphia Female Anti-Slavery Society, and my father is an abolitionist. I once heard Frederick Douglass speak and was so very moved. The murderous beatings the slave breaker Edward Covey gave him when he was still only a boy!"

I hear agitation—perhaps even a rebuke to my japing—in the clatter of her spoon inside the cup.

"Forgive an old instigator," I say, trying to match her earnestness, but a remnant smile of lingering amusement betrays me.

Again her spoon rattles angrily. "The other nurses think you're a bad influence."

"But I'm not, you know."

Her expression softens.

"Am I forgiven?"

"For the moment, but I think we'd better change the subject."

I pause in order to find one. "I was present at an operation yesterday—a cystectomy for a bladder stone the size of that biscuit on your plate."

"You're a beast, Walt Whitman, and I take back my forgiveness!"

Our attention is diverted by a line of ambulances passing in the street. Snow covers the canvas roofs. The sides of the dismal conveyances have been let down to spare the injured the wintery draughts and the bystanders their tender feelings. Snow has collected on the backs of the horses and on the whippletrees.

"They saw the elephant," I say ruefully, using the soldiers' expression for having seen the worst that war can do.

"The poor boys! We'll be meeting some of them soon."

"Wait till the spring offensive; they'll arrive by the boat- and carload."

"Have you attended a rebel soldier?"

"I haven't, though I expect there will be no shortage of them as the war goes on. They will try our patience, Harriet, and our consciences." I'm eyeing this year's calendar tacked on the wall, where the round of days has stalled at Thursday, January 1, 1863, when Lincoln issued the Emancipation Proclamation. Is it to commemorate the day or to curse it? On the western side of Rock Creek, which separates Georgetown from the capital, one cannot be sure on which side of the issue a person stands. "The soul can be a trial and a curse," I say, knowing that I am talking through my hat.

"Surely not!"

"You're very young, Nurse Wright." And Whitman, you're an old dog!

"Not so very young," she says, nibbling a biscuit.

"And very pretty—I speak in the avuncular."

She replies with a crunch of dry biscuit.

"The biscuits here are no better than what the soldiers call 'sheet-iron crackers.'"

"Or 'teeth dullers.'" She shows hers in a smile.

I am fond of Harriet Wright.

"Are you acquainted with the nurse at Union Hospital—the dark-eyed, darkly complected one? She was shaving one of the boys this morning."

"With the thick chestnut hair—no, I'm not. Does she interest Mr. Whitman, who swears he is no Caliban?" Her eyes flash with mischief.

Are you being coquettish, Harriet?

"She has a quality that interests me," I reply with nonchalance.

"I heard that, like you, she came to Washington after Fredericksburg. I believe her home is Concord."

"I know people in Concord. Are you familiar with the name Ralph Waldo Emerson?"

"The abolitionist. My mother and father speak highly of him."

"Emerson called my book 'the most extraordinary piece of wit and wisdom that America has yet contributed.'" I puff myself up expectantly like a bullfrog croaking for a mate.

"I like novels, especially Jane Austen's."

"She writes about manners. Her men and women merely simmer."

"Walter, you have crumbs in your beard," she remarks imperturbably.

"I'll leave them for the birds, since the Lord no longer sees fit to care for the sparrows."

"Does the big old bear have a thorn in its paw?" I glimpse my foolishness in her comical pout.

"The big old bear is a foolish old man," I reply, merrily ringing the jam pot with my spoon.

THE HORSECAR CROSSES ROCK CREEK and rattles down rails laid on Pennsylvania Avenue, toward the Anacostia, the route of my nocturnal rambles with Pete Doyle. The raw wind busses Harriet's cheeks. I am invigorated and would crow like a cockerel were it not for her, who would likely fear my wits have fled. The presence of young people is electric to me. They are unspoiled and unjaded, as I am unspoiled and unjaded, despite the years that have brought gray to my hair and beard, if not wisdom. Leaving wisdom to the philosophers, I am for life vital and manifold. Like the young, I stand plumb in the midst of irrational things, self-balanced for contingencies. I wish this lumbering public conveyance were self-balanced for the contingencies of unpaved streets and lumbago.

"Washington is a magnificent city!" I declare, ignoring the pigs turning up snow with their snouts. "Pediments, entablatures, fluted columns, friezes, immense domes assemble into republican palaces, in which no king or despot dare walk, save at the invitation of the people's representatives."

The rug has slipped from Harriet's lap, and I gallantly restore it.

"There is either too much dirty snow or too much mud in Washington. It draggles my skirts and cakes my shoes. Whenever will they pave the streets and drive the pigs back into the sties?"

"I extol our imperial city, and you carp of muddy skirts. Flyspecks, Harriet! In time, the streets will be paved and the hogs butchered."

"The buildings remind me of tombs and sepulchers. Washington is a necropolis crowded with visitors come to decorate the graves."

"Harriet, you disappoint me! I thought you were a woman of sense and sensibility."

"Fiddlesticks, Walter! Sometimes you forget yourself and your manners."

She is right; nevertheless, I sulk. We ride three or four blocks in silence, our heads turned in opposite directions. The strain having become intolerable, I make an overture to an apology—a catarrhal sound at the back of the throat.

"*Ahem*. Please forgive me, Harriet. I sometimes forget myself and, as you rightly pointed out, my manners. I'm afraid there's a frontier toughness in me that civilization can't soften. I'm like Henry Thoreau, who could be a clodhopper but was a man of extraordinary sympathies. He died last May. In many ways, he was a boy in his enthusiasms. Have you read *Walden; or, Life in the Woods*?"

"Is it an essay?"

"Yes, of book length."

"Then I haven't." She has taken her turn at peevishness and is acquitting herself every bit as well as I did in the role of crank.

I humble myself before youth and beauty. "I *sincerely* beg your pardon."

"I forgive you. You are a bear, and one risks being bitten when keeping a bear company."

"I swear, Harriet, on my mother's eyes, that I will not bite you!"

She laughs, her frowning face unknots, and the day is saved.

We stop at the President's House to watch a regiment of negro soldiers parade in review. Mr. Lincoln watches from the steps. He lifts his hat to them.

"Aren't they wonderful?" cries Harriet above the martial music of a regimental band.

"Superb!" I reply in earnest.

We disembark at the National Bank. The car continues on Pennsylvania Avenue to the Capitol Building. We adjust our mufflers and pull down our hats against the razory wind from the river.

"Are you visiting the wards this afternoon, Walter?" she asks, stamping her feet in an attempt to get the blood flowing. My own feet feel like frozen fish after riding in the cold horsecar.

"I've some business nearby. I may be by this evening. If not, tomorrow, after my toils at the paymaster's."

"I'll be off, then."

I watch her go, lively and vivid, along Seventh Street until she vanishes in the jostling crowd.

MY BUSINESS IS WITH MATHEW BRADY at his photographic gallery on Pennsylvania Avenue, in an ignoble pile of brick and cast-iron colonettes. (How I despise the ersatz!) I take the stairs to the fourth floor and knock neither timidly nor insolently, but with the perfect pitch of a citizen of the Republic.

"Come in!" The voice belongs to a man with little time for civilities.

I enter a large room pierced by skylights that, on this somber January afternoon, are gray. Brady is inspecting a photographic negative through a loupe. A handsome man of middle years, his thin face and aquiline nose are set off by a goatee and mustache. His grizzled hair is brushed back in unruly waves. He takes his time with the glass plate until, satisfied with the result, he turns his bespectacled gaze on me. He suffers from the myopia of an artisan of miniatures, which he was before learning daguerreotypy from Samuel Morse, inventor of the telegraph. America is endued with a multifarious genius; its germ has been coursing through the veins of its people since the Great Migration began to leech Europe of its brains.

"Walt Whitman, I'll be damned!" He sets the loupe aside and turns around in his chair to take me in.

"Mr. Brady, how do you do?" I take my hat off in respect.

"Well enough." He studies my face intently and says, "Our Mr. Gardner caught your likeness to a tee."

Before I left for Fredericksburg, I had my image taken for a pack of *cartes-de-visite* at Brady's Daguerrean Miniature Gallery on Broadway. My face looks as Moses' would have as he beheld the burning bush.

"Your face is remarkable, Whitman. I'd like to photograph it myself, if you have time."

"I'd be delighted." I am not shy of the camera. It may please future readers of *Leaves* to judge what kind of man its author was by his facsimile.

"Set your hulk down in the chair before the light goes."

I do and know to rest my head in the iron clamp behind it to keep it still.

"Shall I shear you while I'm at it?"

I gin my beard with my fingers, admitting my fondness for it.

"It makes you look like an old man."

"It's my eyes that make me look so. The things they've seen."

"The elephant."

"That's so."

Brady wheels a tripod camera toward me. "I can't decide whether you're a saint or a sinner, Walt. Your countenance suggests both."

I am not the poet of goodness only; I do not decline to be the poet of wickedness also.

Brady's head vanishes inside the black drape and then reappears. He reminds me of one of Hogarth's rakes peeking up a trollop's skirts. Expertly, he adjusts the bellows. The camera is beautiful—rectilinear, mahogany, brass-fitted. Not even the Ark of the Covenant, made from a tree felled in the Jordan Valley and overlaid with gold, could have been more beautiful. Brady, too, is beautiful, because there is nothing more so than a man or a woman going about his or her work—each singing what belongs to him or her and to no one else.

"The light is not the best, but it will do," he says. "We are none of us God, who can call it into being."

Or bid Moses to stretch out his hand toward heaven, that there may be darkness over the land of Egypt.

Brady goes to the sink and coats a glass plate with collodion and silver nitrate. He returns with it inside a lightproof holder, which he inserts into the back of the camera. He pulls a wooden slide from the holder. The plate is now vulnerable to the outside world, and no sooner has the lens been uncapped than the silver particles react to the light flooding the dark chamber. He opens his pocket watch and allows the seconds to pass—each ticking loudly in the silent room—until the image on the glass negative reaches a perfection of chiaroscuro. Then he snaps his watch shut and covers the lens with the brass cap. He removes the exposed plate, safe inside the holder, and takes it to the darkroom to develop and fix.

"Not a bad likeness," he says when he rejoins me in the studio.

The sky has darkened, and with it the room. Sleet begins to drum the skylights.

"I caught you in the nick of time," he says, drying his hands.

I lean away from the head clamp and stretch myself until I hear my bones crack.

"I had a visit from William O'Connor yesterday," says Brady.

"I know."

"You know what he wanted?"

"I do."

"It wouldn't have worked. To tell the truth, Walt, I don't think he's dependable."

"If you're hinting that he's fond of the 'oil of gladness,' you're right."

"It shows."

I feel the thrill of betraying a friend, and then the shame of it.

"I've heard shocking things said about your infamous book."

"Most folks do seem to find it so," I say gruffly.

"Most folks like pretty sentiments. You're not a prettifier, Walt Whitman."

"Neither are you," I say, waving a hand at the row of photographs hanging on one wall.

"Bull Run," he says, regarding them critically from the horsehair sofa on which we have settled ourselves to be near the stove. "I nearly got myself killed taking them. I heard hornets rushing past my ears. What're you doing in Washington?"

"I divide my time between purgatory and perdition and am never sure which is which." To his quizzical look, I reply, "I spend half of it making fair copies for the army paymaster and the other half tending the wounded. And sometimes when I get downright confused, I wash out my inkwell with carbolic and write memoranda on the backs of dead boys."

"At Harewood General?"

Death is everywhere.

"Mostly at the old Columbia Armory on the Mall; once a week I visit Union Hospital over in Georgetown."

"You get to see the leftovers."

"Terrible what a two-pounder can do to a man!"

"It's not going to end anytime soon, Walter."

"It'll drag on till we run out of men or places to bury them."

And I found that every place was a burial place; the houses full of life were equally full of death.

I get up and look at the photographs of the Battle of Bull Run, when General McDowell's soldiers were routed and a boodle of folks from Washington—come to see the fun—closed their chair sticks and picnic baskets and fled. We realized that defeating Johnny Reb was going to take a whole lot longer than the six months the big bugs and loudmouths had averred.

"Not exactly picturesque," says Brady, gesturing toward the images of mayhem. "What I can't fathom is the hunger the public has for such sights. They're more popular than pictures of fancy girls in a miners' camp! I need to hire more men to chase

Burnside, McClernand, and Joe Hooker while the rebels chase *them*."

"The people are enraged. They don't want firemen to put out the blaze of their enmity; they want arsonists to inflame it. They won't be satisfied till they've burned the world clean of humankind."

"Could be, Walt, could be—though it's not the kind of thing I'd expect to hear from your mouth. Last time I was in New York, I bought a copy of *Leaves of Grass* on Nassau Street."

"At Fowler & Wells Phrenological Cabinet. They used to keep a chair reserved for me, so that I could watch the people coming and going." (What would phrenologists make of a plaster cast of my big head?)

"It's the eyes and the set of the mouth that reveal the human being, not the bumps on the skull. Gabriel Harrison's daguerreotype reproduced on the frontispiece makes you look like an Adonis."

"What would you say to a collaboration?" I ask impulsively.

"How so?"

"On a book of my experiences in the wards. Your images, my words."

"My images are complete in themselves and require no explanation, just as your poems need no illustrations."

"Mathew, it's not poems only I have in mind, but an amalgamation of words and pictures, to convey a thing too raw for either one to contain. The chloroform sponge, the knife, the saw, the terrible wounds, the amputees with their bloody stumps . . ."

"Walt, your personality is too damn strong—it would sink my pictures to hell!" He points to scenes photographed at the Battle of Shiloh. "They could have been taken by me or any of my assistants. There are no idiosyncrasies of expression there—no artfulness to stand in the way of the viewer and the dead."

There is sense in what he says, so I give up the idea. Bemused, he sits on the sofa and tugs the scraggly end of his mustache. I sit beside him, waiting for him to speak. The sleet has changed to snow, which covers the skylights. A curious twilight settles on the studio, as if we were sitting under polar ice inside one of Robert Fulton's submarines. Or so I imagine, who dares to imagine all.

"Your *Leaves* will survive the war because they're bigger than it is. They'll be making greenhouses and cucumber frames out of my glass-plate negatives."

Swords into plowshares, plowshares into swords. The cradle endlessly rocks between the peace foretold by Isaiah and the lamentations of Jeremiah.

Each lost in his own thoughts, Brady and I sit in the overwhelming gloom, not bothering to turn on the gaslights.

"Sometimes, we pose them," he says, breaking the silence.

"I don't get your meaning."

"We rearrange the dead bodies for the sake of the picture."

"WHY, WHAT A BEAUTIFUL PLAYHOUSE, Walter!" exclaims Nelly O'Connor, sitting beside me in a brocaded seat.

I take in the slender columns supporting the balconies, the unadorned pediment above the president's box overlooking the stage, the chaste decorations painted on the plastered ceiling. It is an elegant interior, but one that speaks plainly of democracy.

"Have you never been to Ford's Theatre?"

"William says we haven't money for treats, and I suppose that's so. He claims the Light-House Board is run by skinflints and party hacks."

"Small men given their head become the biggest despots."

"When we lived in Boston, we went often to the theater."

"Theater can't hold a candle to opera. To hear the prima donna Marietta Alboni declaim in her incomparable contralto, *'Non! — non, non, non, non, non! Vous n'avez jamais, je gage'* in Meyerbeer's *Les Huguenots* roused whirlwinds of feeling within me. Dressed in a crinolined taffeta gown, she resembled the bourdon bell Emmanuel, hanging in the south tower of Notre-Dame, which an ecstatic Quasimodo would ride high above the streets of Paris."

"And what of Jenny Lind?"

"She did not touch me."

Nelly lays a gloved hand on my sleeve.

I offer her a boiled sweet.

She squeezes my wrist.

I peruse the bill and note that a Shakespearean history play is to be staged later this year. "I saw the great tragedian Junius Brutus Booth play Richard III at the Bowery Theatre. Seldom have I seen a more beautifully fashioned man—once he'd taken off the padded hump."

"You've only to look in your mirror, Walt, to see another."

I glance at her. She is an intelligent woman, if plain, whose company I enjoy, but her adoration frightens me. I am for free love and ask no man's leave to copulate. I don't set myself up as a saint, but William—for all he can be an ass—is a friend of long standing and unstinting in his praise of *Leaves*. He calls me "the good gray poet," a designation of which I approve.

"I do hope it's an amusing play!" says Nelly. "Lately, I feel my jaws locked and am afraid my face will wear a perpetual frown."

I foresee a bad end to the O'Connors' marriage.

All heads turn to see Mr. and Mrs. Lincoln take their places in the president's box. Nelly and I contribute to the nearly universal applause. Many Republican gentlemen shout huzzahs, while the ladies wave their handkerchiefs. One secesh dares to hiss and is hurried outside by the scruff of his neck.

Mr. Lincoln stands a moment, shy and grave in expression. He does not appear to enjoy the acclaim. He raises his hand to silence it. He sits beside his wife, Mary Todd. The gaslights are turned low, the curtain rises, and the play begins.

Uninterested in the shenanigans onstage, I peer into the darkness of the president's box, hoping to make out the faces, but they are featureless in the obscurity. Lincoln leans briefly over the railing to have a look at one of the actors or to relieve an ache in his back—who knows? For a moment, I see his face in a ray of light cast by one of the fixtures. The shadows carve a mask terrible to behold. I think that he is a good man, if not the great leader the nation requires in the present emergency. I pity him.

Nelly is finding the play entertaining. How wonderful it must be for her to forget the genteel poverty, the argumentative husband, the dead child, the uncertainties and scarcities of wartime Washington. Go on and laugh, Nelly! If I were not preoccupied, I would indulge in belly laughs worthy of Gargantua. (I am no more fazed by the presence of a senator in a high silk hat than I am by that of the road mender in his leather cap; no man is superior or inferior to me.) Mr. Lincoln, are you laughing? Is it possible for you to forget, if only for three hours, the divided house that fell, as you said it would? Can you forget the incompetent generals, the catastrophic defeats, the sick and wounded men I watched you visit from a corner of my own darkness? Can you forget your grief for young Willie, who died last year of typhoid fever?

After I have seen Nelly to her door, I lie in the "little ease" of my cramped room and recall a November night in 1829, when I went with my parents to hear the Quaker Elias Hicks preach at Morrison's Hotel on Brooklyn Heights. He had torn in two the Religious Society of Friends by proclaiming, "The blood of Christ—the blood of Christ—why, my friends, the actual blood of Christ in itself was no more effectual than the blood of bulls and goats." As the wind rose from the East River and entered through the meetinghouse's plain windows, thrown open to dissipate the charged atmosphere, Hicks exulted in "the light within." He extolled "the fountain of all naked theology, all religion, all worship, all the truth to which you are possibly eligible—namely in yourself and your inherent relations." The most democratic of religionists, he praised the devoutness inside of man's own nature. He spoke with a natural eloquence, an unstudied poetry drawn from a fund within or an atmosphere without, deeper than art, deeper even than proof. His great voice entered me, a ten-year-old boy; it entered and took hold of me as he clapped his black broad-brimmed hat on the lectern and shook out his long white hair. Much later, his rhythms and unself-conscious oratory crept into my verses, as if the serpent in the Garden had been a blessing to our kind instead of a curse. In his style of speaking, which seemed no style at all, Elias Hicks was like Abraham Lincoln, a tall, straight figure, dressed in drab cloth.

This morning as I primped before the mirror, a fragment of last night's dream appeared in the depths of its silvered glass, like a spectral scene in a phénatiscope. Alone in the streetcar, Pete and I were embarked on another of our nocturnal voyages along Pennsylvania Avenue. No driver stood at the dash; no one held the reins. The horses knew the way. They stopped at the President's House. Abe Lincoln boarded and took a seat in back. He wore his old shawl. He said not a word, and Pete and I were silent, as though keeping a vigil. Upon reaching the car barn, I turned in my seat, saying, "End of the line, Father Abraham," only to find that he was not there.

ON SUNDAY, AFTER PETE HAS BEEN to Mass, prayed to the saints, and said his rosaries, we enjoy tramping the bosky paths to visit one of the defensive forts. Our destination this afternoon is Battery Parrott, two miles northwest of Georgetown. The winter freeze has paved November's mud with ice, and during the night, a light snow fell, giving our boots a grip on the iron ground. The oaks stand aside, suffering two mortal men to enter their domain, where the sole breaches of the peace are the gray squirrels' bickering over acorns, the jays' alarms, and—nature being what it is—a red fox's raid on a squatter's chickens, the bloody evidence of which is scattered underneath a juniper bush.

"Seems like Bobby Lee's in hibernation," Pete comments, noting the lull in hostilities.

"I wouldn't depend on it," I say, enjoying the crackle of rimy leaves underfoot. "He's a wily son of a gun and knows how to fight a war a hell of a lot better than our mud turtles do."

"'Fighting Joe' Hooker is top rail," says Pete, picking his teeth with a twig of sassafras.

"It's 'Hooker's Brigade' of camp followers you admire."

"I don't care for that sort," replies Pete with a sniff of disdain, which draws crystals up his nose from his frosted mustache. He blows first one nostril and then the other into the snow to rid them of the icy snuff.

"Maybe so, but you enjoy the idea of any sort of rascality—you with your plug-ugly hat."

Patting his belly with carnal satisfaction, he says, "I am a damned rascal, ain't I?"

We tramp awhile without bothering to work our jaw muscles. I relish the clean, cold air, the resinous odor of the pines, the crunch of snow, and the creaking of the gigantic oaks, whose lofty tops sway in the wind high above us.

"Sounds like a gallows when the body turns to

deadweight and the rope saws against the gibbet," says Pete.

"Any of your people swing?" I ask.

"Not yet."

I pack snow into a facsimile of a crystal ball and pretend to scry his future. "I see a long and rumbunctious life."

"I see smoked Yanks up ahead," Pete replies cheerfully.

The path debouches onto a clearing, half a mile or thereabouts east of the Potomac, seen glaring in the afternoon sun. Trees and brush have been scalped roundabout to deprive the enemy of cover. The battery is nothing fancier than an earthworks overlooking a fording place in the river, where, at low water, the enemy could cross. A dry moat lies at the bottom of the counterscarp, bristling with an abatis of sticks sharp as boars' teeth. Field and siege guns sit behind a dirt parapet. A picket of soldiers is cooking some kind of meat over a wood fire. My eyes and mouth begin to water.

"How are you, Walter?" asks Jenkins, whom I met during my last visit. "Bring any 'shin plasters' with you?"

"You've been paid for the month, you good-for-nothing hornswoggler!"

"That was my government pay," says Jenkins in that appealing way he has of buttering his sarcasm with languidness. "I been expecting the wages of sin Old Scratch promised me."

"I don't work for the Devil," I tell him, putting on a high-and-mighty frown.

"Then you go right to hell and tell Splitfoot you're looking for honest work. Tell him you're tired of Lyman Hapgood's chisel."

"Want some possum, Walt?" asks another young soldier. "Wendell shot it this morning."

"I'm sick of army 'coosh'!" says Wendell, referring to hardtack fried in bacon grease.

"We got busthead to wash it down with," says a soldier missing a piece of one ear. "It'll melt the fillings in your mouth."

"I'll have a swallow," says Pete, smoothing his sparse mustache with his thumb.

The soldier fills a tin cup with corn whiskey and hands it to him.

"What brings you here?" inquires Jenkins as he squints through the smoke at the blistering meat spitted on his bayonet.

"We felt like bumming." The smell of roasting meat reminds me that I haven't eaten since breakfast. "Get the hospital stink out of my nose and the smell of horses out of my friend Doyle's."

Pete nods amiably toward the men, and they return a mute but friendly greeting.

"Better get upwind of Meyer," advises the soldier with the nicked ear as he fans the air with his cap.

"He's been doing the quick step all morning. God Almighty, he does stink!"

"It comes from eating dog," says Wendell.

"Shit, I don't eat dog!" declares Frank Meyer, a private with a nervous twitch in one eye. "It's that old spring—the water smells."

"That water's sweet as a pretty gal's mouth!" objects Wendell, who strikes me as the contrarious sort. "It's your rotten gut, Frank, does the mischief."

"'Yahweh smote him in his bowels, and his bowels fell out by reason of his sickness,'" intones a gaunt soldier from Ohio, who was likely reared in a revival tent.

"We got a jarful of Meyer's farts saved up for Jefferson Davis. They'll exfluncticate the son of a bitch!"

"Fuck you, Wendell—you, Jeff Davis, and Bobby Lee's horse!" shouts Meyer, pleased to be the center of attention.

"I wouldn't mind another taste of corn," says Pete, indifferent to the palaver, which I am enjoying and wishing that it could be set among my verses.

"Seen any graybacks?" I ask, watching the ghost of my breath writhe in the ice-cold air.

"None this side of the river, though the lice is plentiful."

"Then I'll stand here awhile and fumigate in the smoke," I say, feeling, by the power of suggestion, nits crawling underneath my shirt.

"Your brother was at Fredericksburg, wasn't he?" asks Jenkins.

"He was."

"All right, is he?"

"He's in Tennessee with the Fifty-first New York."

"Fredericksburg was a bollocks!" spits a flinty sergeant named Delby. "We were like an ox that got stuck halfway through a fence, torn by dogs, front and rear, without a fair chance to gore one way or kick the other."

"Yes, sir, it was," I admit.

"You got no call to call me 'sir'! I don't have pumpkin rinds on my shoulders or chicken shit on my sleeves." He kicks a loose stone down the slope. I watch it jump over the lip of the moat and come to rest against a pointed stick. I imagine a Johnny Reb impaled on it and shiver.

"I saw the damnedest thing one night at Fredericksburg. I was lying in the mansion yard, waiting for somebody to die, so I could take his bed, when the sky lit up with green and reddish streamers, all shimmery like," says Jenkins quietly, as if he were again watching the atmospheric show. "It was real pretty."

"I saw it, too," says the soldier with the disfigured ear. "And it were pretty!"

"I recall the night I was lying in Miller's cornfield at Sharpsburg, after Lee just about annihilated our entire company. The worst off of the wounded began to glow green, like a ship's rigging will sometimes with Saint Elmo's fire. It gave me a fright!" remarks Delby in a subdued voice.

"'The heavens declare the glory of God; and the firmament showeth His handiwork!'" cries the Bible-thumper.

Jenkins slides the smoking possum from his bayonet onto a length of old sheet metal. "Care for a piece, Walter?"

Seeing that there is hardly enough to go around, I decline. "We had bread and salt horse on the way here."

With a jackknife, Jenkins proceeds to carve the animal.

"I could do with a little meat," says Peter, looking up from his third cup of whiskey.

I glower at him. "Just a morsel for my friend."

Jenkins obliges with a slice of belly meat.

"Thank you kindly."

"Well, gents, time we were going," I say, glancing at the sky, as if the hour were written there. "Say, I brought you boys a few treats." I take out of my rucksack a pack of playing cards, a dozen crisp Virginia Beauties, dipping, chaw, and smoking tobacco, barley sugar candies, some new handkerchiefs, and a harmonica, whose previous owner left it behind when he climbed into Heaven to take up the Aeolian harp. "Anyone care for a mouth organ?"

"I do," says grum Sergeant Delby.

I hand it to him, and he begins to play, cupping his hands around it to make it moan.

"Play 'Softly Now the Light of Day,'" requests the Ohioan.

"Hell no!" shouts Jenkins. "Play 'Effie, the Maid of the Hill.'"

"Don't know it," says the sergeant, knocking the spit from the instrument onto his palm.

"Boys, much as I'm enjoying the repartee, my friend and I have to get back to the city."

"Mind how you go, Walt," calls Jenkins after me. "And tell Lyman Hapgood that the tanner will give me twice as much for my hide than what the army pays—camp itch and all!"

The sergeant sounds a derisive note on the harmonica.

INSTEAD OF RETURNING THROUGH the woods, we go by way of the Potomac. We pass snow-bandaged stumps left by the army after cutting down the pines around Battery Parrot. The ruined landscape is as pathetic as a battlefield yet to be harvested of its dead and dying men. What grievous wounds must the earth endure before this war is finished? What death's-heads will spring from Hydra's teeth to harrow the future? I, who have been vouchsafed glimpses of the future, cannot answer.

Below the heights of Fredericksburg, the corpses

are gone from the slaughter pen. Rain has cleansed the ground of gore. Rid of the last particle of corruption, the Rappahannock goes once more about its business, which is to flow everlastingly from the Blue Ridge Mountains to Chesapeake Bay. The river before us also has a course to follow: It rises in the Appalachians and, having gathered tributary waters, empties into the bay, which mixes its element with that of the Atlantic. In rivers, there is an inevitability that gainsays our belief in freedom. As their atoms travel to predestined ends, so must mine flow onward until they mingle my essence with the rest.

Pete trips over a stump and falls flat.

"That's what comes of drinking busthead on the Sabbath—God blast your heathen heart, Doyle!"

He gets to his feet, dusts the snow from his hands, and sways a moment till he finds his balance. "I'm not corned!" he replies, affronted. He licks his greasy mustache. "It's the possum belly that done it."

"You couldn't walk a straight line if there were a quart of rye and a Dutch gal at the other end! Or a gal-boy if that be your pleasure."

"Fuck all!"

He gets under way again in the exaggerated manner of the soused, which is picturesquely termed a "Virginia fence" for its crookedness. I notice his hat on the ground. I fetch it and knock the snow from the crown. "Your lid," I say, taking him by the arm to arrest him in his onward stagger.

"Much obliged."

"Don't give it a second thought."

"Then I won't." He eyes his crusher critically, frowns at a grease spot, puts it on, adjusts the tilt of it, and finishes the operation with an emphatic thump of his palm. "How do I look?"

"Like a Broadway dude."

"Thank you very much!"

"Now, shall we be on our way?"

"Give me a minute." He drops to his knees in the snow, lowers his head, his hat falls off, and he vomits into it. "Would you look at that!" he exclaims in astonishment, like someone who beholds a miracle.

"You can sure pile on the agony!"

"That was a three-dollar hat." He is genuinely perplexed by this latest instance of God's inscrutable will.

I offer him my hand, he takes it, and I pull him to his feet. "Feeling better?"

"My ears are froze!" He is cupping them with his gloved hands.

"Take my scarf." He winds it under his chin and over his ears and knots it on top of his head. "You look fit to be laid out and keened over."

He gives his beloved, now befouled, hat a kick and once again makes for the river—this time without the staggers. Following him, I try to set down my boots where he has broken the crust, but my stride quickly overtakes his. We reach the bank of the Potomac and head toward Mason's Island, four miles to the south. The shore is laced with ice, but in the channel, the turbid water hurries onward to the bay. I nibble a piece of hardtack. I eat a little snow to quench my sudden thirst. Sapped of vitality, Pete trudges in silence behind me. Just as well, since I am in no mood to hear him grumble.

What's this now, Walt—an old man's tears?

No, it is merely the headwind, freighted with particles of ice, which makes me weep.

I think you have entered the famous slough. See! from your dead lips the ooze exuding at last!

I am shivering with cold, and yet I feel sweat trickle from my armpits. Emerson hated the word, which I used in Leaves. *Perhaps his are less aromatic than mine. No dainty dolce affetuoso I. Words should walk, weep, kiss, do the male and female act.*

The handsome nurse with richly colored hair whom I twice saw in the wards steps from the darkness onto the dimly lighted stage of my fancy. "Mr. Whitman, you're wanted," she says gravely.

"Wanted by whom?" I reply with a faint, quivering intonation.

She puts her finger to her lips and bids me hush.

I follow her outside into the falling snow, where Pete is waiting with the horsecar. She climbs aboard, sits, and gestures that I should sit beside her. Gallantly, I cover her lap with a buffalo rug. The driver flaps the lines, and the horses walk on down Pennsylvania Avenue. We stop at the President's House. Except for light flickering at the windows of his bedchamber, the house lies in darkness. The dark nurse and I hurry inside and quickly mount the stairs. Two tall candles light the president's body, contending with the deep shadows that delineate his rawboned face. His sunken eyes are closed. Without a word, we prepare the corpse. I tie my scarf under the jaws to keep the mouth shut. Abraham Lincoln's speech-making days are finished, unless there be secesh angels and Copperheads in heaven for him to rail against.

"Walt!" Peter is tugging at my sleeve. "Walter!"

"What is it?" I ask, starting from my daydream.

"There!" he says, pointing to the riverbank, where the snow is peppered with crows.

The shape is unmistakable. I have seen its like many times before. It is the same as that of a dead man covered by bedclothes. I shake my head; I rub my face with snow. I hurry toward the telltale heap, waving my hat to disperse the scavenging birds. By the river, I kneel and brush the snow from the purplish face. His raggedy clothes are stiff.

"A colored man," says Pete, stooping beside me.

"He's not much older than a boy. He must've drowned trying to cross."

"A contraband," says Pete, fingering his chin.

The Confiscation Act of 1862 classified fugitive slaves as "contraband" liable to seizure by the Union army, which has no legal obligation to return "spoils of war." By insisting on their status as things, the runaways were freed. A clever ruse, if demeaning.

"He came damn close to emancipating himself!" I remark savagely enough to make Pete jump. "What'll we do with him?"

"I bet they got picks and shovels at Battery Parrott."

"I doubt they'll stir for a dead negro." Musing, I watch the river breathe out mist. "Tell you what: Let's give him back to the river. The current can take him where it will."

"I don't much care for the idea, Walt. Seems to me even a colored man has a right to a final resting place."

"The dead have no more rights than the living do!" I growl as I recollect a November day in 1842, at the old Baptist burial ground, when money once again beggared decency.

At the time, I was a correspondent for the *Aurora*. Anson Herrick, one of the publishers, sent me to the Delancey Street graveyard, where a widow was said to be standing guard, with a loaded pistol, over the remains of her husband and child. The snakes and jackals of the Hudson Fire Insurance Company had bought the ground to divide and sell as house lots. When I arrived, their hired men had already opened the graves with pickaxes. With a shiver, I saw the fleshless bones and skulls of Manhattan's antique dead. They lay helter-skelter in heaps, the color of old piano keys. As a boy, I'd seen the like cast up by Wallabout Bay, near the Brooklyn Navy Yard. Father said that they were the bones of patriots left to molder inside sunken British prison hulks. The place is known as "Potter's Field" because of the many bodies that wash up there. The bones of more recently departed Baptists from the Lower East Side—uprooted and disgraced—were white, the marrow moist and spongy, their perfect concinnity intact. I pictured infants and young children carried early to the grave by some malignancy or accident. In one lathwork of heavy bones, I saw a man who could have raised a rooftree on his back or hauled a keelboat out of a dead calm with his muscled arms. And on a dainty frame, my fancy hung the sweet form of a girl who might have inclined her swanlike neck in proud acknowledgment of the admiring glances of young men. I, too, would have glanced admiringly, giving beauty its due.

I watched the widow's anger turn to grief and the curious bystanders turn indignant when the constables arrived and took her away. I knew then that nothing is consecrated that cannot be deconsecrated, that there is nothing our kind will not outrage, and that the notion of eternal rest is contingent on the appetites of land speculators. From yawning graves, the dead are given up prematurely. To say we rise again as grass is to say nothing of the weeds and the mower and the parching heat. I cannot say for sure that to die is not a misery.

Pete kneels in the snow and prays. "'We therefore commit his body to the deep, looking for the general Resurrection in the last day, and the life of the world to come, through our Lord Jesus Christ; at whose second coming in glorious majesty to judge the world, the sea shall give up her dead; and the corruptible bodies of those who sleep in him shall be changed.'" Only God knows from what depths he dredged up words reserved for a burial at sea, unless they had been impressed upon him, when, as an eight-year-old boy from Limerick, he made the ocean crossing.

Let Peter take comfort where he can and with whatever words have been given him to say. We are weak vessels of a potter who has yet to learn his trade. We are dashed against stones and break, or we break at the slightest touch. Our sole certainty is that we reach our separate ends in pieces, which may or may not be made whole again. I will keep such glum thoughts to myself, since they are unbecoming to a man who sings.

You should teach yourself to croak, old man, for the times are lamentable!

I hold the frozen body of the nameless black man in my arms, as Samuel did a lamb to sacrifice to his God; as Mary, the mother of God, held her crucified son when he was taken down from the gibbet; or as

Achilles did the body of Patroclus, whom Ajax slew at the Theban gates.

The sun is low on the horizon. The sky and river are leaden now that the light is going. The wind bites, like a swarm of blackflies. With the young man in my embrace, I step out onto the ice to see if it will bear my weight, and his. Satisfied, I walk to the open channel and lay the body in the rushing water. The water accepts it without reverence or ceremony. The elements are indifferent to our kind, whose lives are brief. The body—even that once belonging to Dives, who dressed it in purple but was unmoved by the beggar Lazarus—it, too, ends up destitute. By the time the Four Horsemen ride, it will have been picked clean.

I glance over my shoulder at Peter, who is still on his knees. The scarf knotted on top of his head makes him look foolish. I regard the river. Already the body has gone. Straining my eyes to see in the uncertain light, I glimpse the corpse. Brutal word, it renders what was human into meat. I glimpse the man as he slips toward the unseen bay and, beyond, the farther ocean. His body is carried, as though on the strong backs of porters. Tomorrow or the day after, he will pause in his outbound journey as the ocean currents vie to claim him. By one means or another, he will go forth not to multiply, but to make his end. Perhaps the water will enfold and carry him to Florida's viridian coast, where he will rest amid red mangroves, or to Saint-Domingue, where Toussaint L'Ouverture and his enslaved comrades cast out their French masters. Perhaps the water will take the drowned man north, following the Drinking Gourd, as the slave song has it, where he will enter New York Bay, pass through the Narrows, and ascend the East River to Hell Gate or the Hudson to its source, Lake Tear of the Clouds.

> His beautiful body is borne in the
>   circling eddies . . . . it is
>   Continually bruised on rocks,
> Swiftly and out of sight is borne the
>   brave corpse.

The iron ground gives up its ghost. The sap is frozen in the elms. Even now the river is soldering an icy integument. They augur death for North and South alike as the gray shroud of winter lengthens. The armies of union and disunion will undergo the various transformations of mortality. Washington City will fall, if not to our enemies, then to time. In time Richmond will be as Thebes. The primeval forest will crack the foundation stones and the rooftrees. Beasts and creeping things will inherit the Earth.

No, Whitman, it's sickness that is speaking and not despair! You have breathed too much poison. You need an emetic or a purge and a couple days' rest. Let the surgeon lay the blue pill on your tongue; it is more efficacious than the cracker of the Sacrament. Earth has wobbled, but it will right itself again. Men cannot be forever at one another's throats!

I see where the dead man goes. He goes to Africa, where he will arise beneath a copper sun and walk the dazzling streets of an ancient kingdom—his oiled hair plaited with gold and his neck, which once an iron collar chafed, adorned by a necklace of precious stones. Perchance he will return to these United States—this Egypt of his bondage. Not content to remain in princely exile, he will return and claim what rightfully belongs to him. For too long, he has been denied his birthright. His patience at an end, he will take his portion. My poem, which comprehends multitudes, shall make room for him among its verses, which will not end.

My *Leaves* are verdant and everlasting. Everywhere they push and shove, as a seedling does to take its place in the sun or as a man or a woman does to breathe his or her share of the universal oxygen. My verses have the strength of multitudes. They break through the obdurate earth, like the tines of a harrow, to bring forth the flower in its season.

Men and women of the future, be content. Whoever is not yet in the grave will have all that is necessary. The black race and that of the aboriginals, as well as the white, you will have what was promised at the inception.

In my poems, I shall deliver Lazarus from the tomb, and his body will be rid of every particle of corruption, for the body is neither poor nor destitute. Whether fleshed or flensed, I say that it is holy—a chariot of fire that will be consumed by the glorious effulgence of its final day.

LOUISA MAY ALCOTT

Washington City
DECEMBER 13, 1862–JANUARY 21, 1863

"*Y*ou're a shameless ass, Walt Whitman, and I am not the least in awe of you!"

I went into the ward after counting sheets and bandages and found you hovering over a young soldier whose arm had been blown off. You looked up and fixed me with a stare, as if to press me between the pages of your obnoxious book. I recognized you as the swaggering egotist whose engraved likeness appeared on the frontispiece of *Leaves of Grass*. Your manner there reeked of affectation. You'd have us believe you are "one of the roughs," when the truth is you're an idler in love with his own "nonchalance." Your conceit is boundless, your "barbaric yawp" twaddle, and your self-aggrandizement—

You have no idea how vexed Mr. Emerson was to see his private letter to you published in the *New-York Tribune*, and, in an even more flagrant breach of his trust, his generous words of praise—"I greet you at the beginning of a great career"—emblazoned on the spine of the second edition of the book. On the *spine*! That good man Henry Thoreau—why, even my harebrained father, whom you'd beguiled at Taylor's saloon, wearing your baggy trousers tucked into your boots—was appalled!

I expect brass from P. T. Barnum, whose preposterous congeries are twice as amusing as your "inventories of democracy," as I've heard Mr. Emerson complain of your interminable lists. Henry T. joked that your poetic method is to put *Wilson's Business Directory of New York City* through the wringer and collect the dribble. One of the roughs, indeed! You're a humbug! I don't care a fig leaf if you swim with a boodle of naked "camerados," but I won't stand for a strutting cockalorum.

"Coming, Mrs. Ropes." I call in answer to the matron's summons.

Hannah Ropes oversees the army nurses at Union Hospital, where fate has delivered me, abetted by the cars from Boston to New London, a packet to Jersey City, and a second train that took me past winter hills white with tents. All summer in Concord, I fretted. Louisa, you must do something more useful than knitting socks, picking lint for bandages, and dashing off blood and thunder tales for *Frank Leslie's Illustrated Newspaper* to keep the pathetic family Alcott afloat. One couldn't buy a yard of cloth, a peck of meal, or a bottle of ink without hearing news of casualties suffered at Shiloh, Second Bull Run, Gaines' Mill, or the Union's Pyrrhic victory at Antietam. Eighteen sixty-two was a funeral in Concord. The papers supplied the crepe, black with doleful tidings from the battlefields and engravings made from photographs taken by Mathew Brady and his wet-plate sodality. A bevy of village girls followed in the footsteps of Florence Nightingale, which had led her from the Crimea to the English workhouses, where she sent the incompetent "Sarah Gamps" packing. I was determined to do likewise in the District of Columbia. I long to be a man, but as I can't fight, I will content myself working for those who can.

Louisa, you must go! I told myself. Father will have to take himself in hand and find gainful employment to keep Mother and sisters from going under. I've done enough! No doubt he will sponge off poor Mr. Emerson. There's no more Henry Thoreau—how I miss him!—to bring the impoverished Alcotts melons, huckleberries, and the odd pickerel. They shan't starve! Oh, but I wish for once Father would interest himself in worldly matters! It's a shame to be poor when there's no reason for it. (Fruitlands nearly did us in.) How many sentimental romances has indigence obliged me to write for money? Money has me scurrying like a pismire dragging an enormous crumb of stale cake up an anthill. These hack tales I seem doomed to write would stagger Sisyphus. Was there ever such rubbish as this:

> Pacing down the garden paths with
> Agnes at my side, our steps were arrested
> by a sudden sight of Effie fast asleep
> among the flowers. She looked a flower
> herself, lying with her flushed cheek pil-
> lowed on her arm, sunshine glittering on
> the ripples of her hair, and the changeful
> lustre of her dainty dress. Tears moist-
> ened her long lashes, but her lips smiled
> as if in the blissful land of dreams she
> had found some solace for her grief.

Such prose would purge a sick man's guts quicker than ipecac.

"Nurse Alcott, you're woolgathering!"

"I'm sorry, Matron."

"This afternoon, Captain Fenzil will be amputat-ing a leg. I want you to observe. Do you think you can do so without fainting?"

"I'm sure I can, Matron." I'm sure of no such thing.

"I want no fussing."

"Matron?"

"Well?"

"The visitor in the ward, who sat by Corporal Riggins's bed—the big red-faced, bearded man wear-ing a wine-colored suit."

"I take it you mean Mr. Whitman."

"Is he a friend of the corporal?" I ask.

"Mr. Whitman is a deputy of the Christian

Commission. We sometimes see him here, but mostly he visits Armory Square Hospital. Do you know the gentleman, although I believe he is not considered one? His manners and way of speaking are coarse."

"He and my father are acquainted. I never met the man myself."

"Superintendent Dix suspects him of disreputable behavior."

He's a bamboozler, a boor, and a tedious poet, but no bugger. "I'm sure, Matron, that he's not a reprobate."

"I'm told he has written an immoral book."

"It was praised by Ralph Waldo Emerson." How perverse, I think, that I should suddenly feel called upon to defend it!

"I have my doubts about that person also. He's said to be an atheist."

"He's an ordained minister," I retort, bristling. During meetings of the Transcendental Club, I've heard Mr. Emerson say that God is one's own soul carried to perfection. His theology would sound alarming to Hannah Ropes, who in every aspect, save a blinkered view of spiritual matters, is selfless and devoted. How I loved to hear the Concord sages argue the philosophies of Plato, Kant, and Hegel while I served them tea and cake!

"A Unitarian!" She sniffs, as if something foul has passed under her nose. "And didn't he give up preaching altogether?"

"To *write!*" I reply emphatically, as though one has merely to utter the word of that most august vocation to silence all complaint.

"Writing is all well and good, Nurse, but we are judged not by our words but by what we do. That goes for you as well, Miss Alcott."

"Doesn't Mr. Whitman do good by his visiting?" Again, I amaze myself by defending the man whom, only minutes before, I faulted as a crass opportunist.

"He does; however, his motives are dubious." Unaware of the movement of her hands, she adjusts the bosom of her plain gray dress with a most unmatronly tug.

"In what way 'dubious'?" Louisa May, will you never learn to shut the barn door before the jackass gets loose?

"There has been talk. . . ." Her voice trails off into the tantalizing silence reserved for religion and malicious gossip.

There will always be talk; it's one thing we can count on in this life. And because people love to speak ill of the dead, slander, backbiting, and slurs continue beyond the grave. They constitute our immortal part.

"Fiddlesticks!"

"You are very young, Miss Saucebox," says the matron in a voice as starched as her cap.

Not so young as all that! I glance at the bloodstains on her apron. They're a warrant of her experience in matters thus far alien to me. I'd guess that

Mrs. Ropes is ten years my senior. To her, I must seem a girl more suitable for parlors and ladies' seminaries than reeking casualty wards. I allow I am naïve when it comes to the sight of men's innards and their sexes, but I've shoveled, hoed, raked, stooped, picked, and done what ladies seldom do. I was ten years old at the time of Father's brainstorm—an experiment in poverty and starvation, as if those subjects needed our empirical research to prove how onerous, mortifying, and destructive they are to the human spirit. Communal undertakings like Fruitlands can put a zealot into an early grave.

My ass of a father is a darling of the Transcendentalists—even of dear Mr. Emerson, who has long been the almoner of the Alcott family. Father lectures publicly on Life but has never bothered much about making a living. Even when he ran the Temple School on Tremont Street—laudable and enlightened as it may have been—the books were never balanced, and the pathetic family Alcott was forever in arrears. Mother has had to take that burden on herself—and I, too, for whom money is the end and aim of my mercenary existence. I want to write about the great themes of human nature and not about the palpitating hearts of lovelorn ladies sighing in their boudoirs. The tribulations of the Pathetic Family would make a capital book. May I live to see it done! I'm resolved to take Fate by the throat and shake a living out of her.

I've worked myself into a wrathy temper, as

Henry used to say. Henry Thoreau, I miss you! If only you knew how much I wished to be the consort of your days and nights (until Mr. Emerson— Waldo—became my master and the God of my idolatry). I ought to have been more forward on those happy afternoons, idling on Walden Pond, in your blue-and-green boat, while you played your cherrywood flute.

"Miss Alcott, your mind is miles away!"

"I beg your pardon, Mrs. Ropes. I was thinking of Mr. Whitman." You can be such a liar, Louisa! "I've heard that he pays for the small presents he gives to the men with his own money," I say to nettle her.

"Mr. Whitman does do some good," says the matron begrudgingly. "As a volunteer."

Putting on a serious face, I wait to hear the *but* or the *nevertheless,* which is certain to follow.

"Nevertheless—"

There it is, Louisa: the eternal quibble that turns truth to drivel.

"As a deputy of the Christian Commission, his morals must be above reproach."

"What time will Mr. Fenzil begin?" I ask to get the matron going down another path.

"Heaven's, child, this isn't a railway depot! There are no timetables here, except as urgency dictates. Arms and legs take precedence over fingers and toes. See that you're by the surgery between supper and dinner. And you'd better take along a bottle of spirits of ammonia, in case you get feeling puny. The first amputation is overwhelming."

"Matron, at the moment, we are overwhelmed with lice," I say with the impertinence that Henry found so endearing in me and my mother finds so very trying.

"At Union Hospital, they're all Lincolnites," Mrs. Ropes remarks with laudable irony. "So don't fret yourself."

I ARRIVED JUST BEFORE THE WOUNDED of Fredericksburg washed up in a bloody tide on the capital. Of dithering General Burnside's 115,000 soldiers, nearly 13,000 Union men and boys had either gone to their unhallowed graves beside the Rappahannock River or—after lingering in a Washington hospital—would soon be given their portion of contested earth, in the government lot. Seeing the unending line of farmers' market carts loaded with human perishables, I hid in a linen closet, no longer feeling like the Lady with the Lamp and wishing to be back in a Concord parlor, opining on the glories of war. The matron chivied me out from my covert and set me to washing blood and excrement from a dozen bodies in which the fire had not yet gone out. One gets used to Death's livery.

Or not.

I did, and have come to *enjoy* it. Forgive the word; it's hardly apt. Let's say I'm fulfilled by my ability to acquit myself with efficiency and compassion. I believe that I'm a favorite of the men, who take comfort in having their bodily wants seen to by a woman resembling a massive cherub in a red headscarf. The trick is to jolly them and not let them see your disgust. The stench is appalling! The first thing every morning, I throw open the sashes to air out the place, regardless of how the boys grouse at the wintery draughts. (My attic room is furnished with five broken panes, to save me the trouble of opening the window. I've hung a bedsheet over it to baffle the cold and the gaze of curious soldiers billeted across the street.) A more perfect pestilence box than Union Hospital I never saw—draughty, damp, and dirty. Rats and roaches, which one can easily mistake for currants, are the only living things that flourish here.

Since one o'clock this afternoon, I've been dressing wounds, changing soiled sheets, and thinking how I might convert the hideous sights and smells engulfing me into stories. The novice who wishes to elbow her way among the fat priests cracking wise at literature's altar rail must—we're told—write of her own experience of the world, be it as small and humble as a pantry full of peach preserves.

"Nurse Alcott?"

"Yes, Doctor." I presume that it's Mr. Fenzil, the surgeon, who has pulled me up sharp. He is a handsome man in his middle years, fair-haired and bearded, whose gaze is cold. Maybe not so cold as severe. He gives the impression that he can see the hooks and eyes at the back of my corset and disapproves of it. His penetrating eyes are enough to make me shiver! Whitman's, which probed and vexed me while I shaved a wounded officer, are gray, red-rimmed, and moist. Waldo's are blue, wise, and a little sad. Henry's—good grief, I can't recall the color of my dear Henry's eyes!

"Follow me," says the surgeon gruffly.

We go behind a screen at the far end of the ward, where thin daylight manages to squeeze through the grimy windows sufficiently to make an operation feasible, if augmented by a smoky lamp or two. A nurse has given the patient a chloroform sponge to breathe before Mr. Fenzil begins to saw.

Beside the wounded man's cot, a table has been laid with a bone saw, scalpels, bistouries, curettes for scraping and cleaning, bone nippers, sutures, bandages, and a tourniquet. The man on the table has lapsed into blessed oblivion. I pray that he will not wake until the ghastly business is over. The doctor addresses his small audience—a surgical assistant, an older nurse plain as a shovel, a porter propped up by a broom, and me—in a lackluster tone, as if sawing off a man's leg were hardly worth the exercise of his vocal cords. I don't expect oratory; this is a hospital and not the House of Representatives, and Fenzil is not Henry Clay or Daniel Webster. But for so awful an occasion, you'd think the surgeon would show some enthusiasm as he prepares to fraction a man.

"You need to cut quickly, so the patient won't die of shock. When men are stacked up and waiting for the saw, I let the fresh wound of the amputation granulate—in other words, I leave it to scab, as the veins and tissue mend. If I have time to do more than any butcher can, I cut two long flaps of skin and tissue, then fold and sew them into a 'fish mouth.' Since this boy is my last for the day, I'll give him a nice rounded stump. If he survives the operation and the 'hospital gangrene,' Dr. Mott"—he indicates the assistant, who is delicately probing his ear canal with a matchstick—"will measure him for a Jewett's leg. Otherwise, the carpenter can measure him for a pine box."

Fenzil takes up the saw and wipes the blade on his blood-spattered apron. He gives the soldier's blasted leg the same coldly calculating look he'd used moments before to appraise me.

"Can't you sprinkle morphine powder on the wound?" I ask, not caring if he considers me impertinent. In Concord, I'm famous for my impertinences. One must be forward if not to be pushed back and held down by adversity. Oh, Father, if you'd only work instead of opining and philosophizing! Your sublime thoughts cannot raise a single ear of corn from seed, drive a nail in a sagging privy door, or relieve Mother of her drudgery!

"Surgery requires more subtlety and skill than emptying a chamber pot," he chides me.

Here is yet another ass! I say to myself, furious at the vanity of men. Only my lovely Henry was never known to bray, however much he liked to crow to wake his neighbors up.

"Hold him down!" orders the righteous Mr. Fenzil. The assistant, the nurse, and I each take a limb and pull, as if we meant to disjoint the man. Even the porter puts down his broom and lies across the soldier's chest. "Not on his lungs, man! I don't want him dying of asphyxia! You there, don't yank so hard on the drumstick! He's not a turkey."

Fenzil commences to saw. The soldier's eyes open and bulge in their sockets; he bucks and judders; he gasps, taking a deep, shuddering breath that comes out in a scream. He subsides onto the cot and faints about the same time that his leg falls to the floor. The porter picks it up—with commendable *nonchalance*, Mr. Whitman—and drops it into a pail. I'm resolved not to turn away from the monstrous proceedings. I'm determined not to be sick. I do, however, feel near to fainting and so give my nose to the spirits phial.

"Give him some more chloroform, Dr. Mott."

Mott does, and the patient sinks into the sediment of consciousness, like a mudfish.

Fenzil is moistening the sutures in his mouth to make them pliable, then shortly begins to stitch the flaps of skin he cut while I was indisposed. Blood covers his apron, hands, and wrists. His fingernails look as if he were digging potatoes. Finished, he leaves the mess to a colored sister and the instruments to his assistant, who takes them to a washtub for a rinse. One would think that the doctors' aprons, stained and stiff with gore, would be burned in the incinerator, along with the dirty bandages. But the idea of contagion is said to be bunkum.

In the summer of 1857, I left Boston to help my mother and sisters nurse the Halls, who were living in a room above a pigpen, in Walpole, New Hampshire, which the landlord had not bothered to clean of filth. Whether by breathing miasma or by contagion, May and Lizzie caught scarlet fever from the Hall children. Two of them died, and so did our Lizzie. It does make me wonder if surgeons ought not to wash their hands, regardless of sniffy Dr. Meigs's declaration that "doctors are gentlemen, and gentlemen's hands are clean."

"Nurse Alcott."

"Doctor!" His sudden appearance on the hospital's back porch startles me. I've taken to sitting here when my work is done to purge my lungs with cold night air. I picture them as a pair of sponges that have given their lives to scrubbing floors. I'm no stranger to hard work; my father's disdain for it has made me a navvy.

Fenzil sits beside me on the low brick wall while a brawny man wearing a leather smock carries a bucket of coal into the hospital kitchen and, after a clunk and rattle, carries out the ashes in the same bucket. If only human intercourse were as easily transacted!

"You disappointed me," says Fenzil, crossing his legs, a gesture that he performs more elegantly than he did the amputation.

"How so?" My body stiffens; my nerves grow taut. I picture removing the doctor's head with his own bone saw and sending it to P. T. Barnum in a hatbox.

"It amuses me to have a callow nurse observe an amputation."

"No doubt you expected me to swoon away at the first drop of blood."

"You did not swoon, Miss Alcott. The only pleasure you gave me was to see your nose rooting at the spirits bottle."

"I did not come all the way from Concord to please you, Mr. Fenzil!" I speak with enough heat to see the ghost of my breath fraying in the wintery air.

"Why did you come, if not to find a husband among the wreckage?"

I have no wish for a husband when I am saddled with a child-father. "A husband is an anchor around a woman's neck."

"I believe you're in earnest, Miss Alcott."

"I am! I will not be bridled." The man is insufferable.

"What's that you're reading?" he asks as he takes a cigar from a leather case. "*Mrs. Beeton's Book of Household Management*, I'd hazard, or one of those sensational tales penned for hysterical young ladies."

I bristle on both accounts, especially the latter, since I am guilty of writing such tales. "A novel by Anthony Trollope."

"The Englishman." Fenzil takes the book rudely from my hands and flips through the pages. "Trollope doesn't hold a candle to Mr. Dickens. May I smoke?"

"Please do; it will fumigate my lungs."

He gives me back my book, beheads his cigar, and spits the end over his shoulder. "Did you ever read any of Edgar Allan Poe's things?"

"I have."

He strikes a lucifer on a brick, waves the sulfur stink away, lights his cigar, and smokes contentedly as the conversation advances by fits and starts. "He knew how to write! I thrill to his tales of weird events and of minds so fretful and self-aware that they cannot but crack under the strain, like the foundation of the House of Usher, or crumble into dust, like the desiccated flesh of M. Valdemar! What do you think of them?"

"I admire them."

"I knew the man," he says offhandedly.

"Poe?" I'm surprised, although maybe I ought not

to be, since Fenzil seems as chilly a man as I imagine the master of gothic horror to have been. The doctor strikes me as an intense, perverse, and forbidding person—no matter how elegantly he crosses his legs.

"We were often together during the winter of '44, when he was living in Philadelphia."

My curiosity gets the better of me, and I ask to hear more.

"At the time, I worked for Thomas Dent Mütter, a surgeon of great renown, at Jefferson Medical College. I was nineteen when he hired me to look after his freaks and fetuses, brains and morbid organs laid up in jars like piccalilli. It took some getting used to, that raree show, but I persevered and became useful to him. It was Dr. Mütter who paid my tuition to attend the medical college, from which, in due course, I was graduated. I owe him much, as you can see."

I don't know what I'm supposed to see unless it is the strain against his waistcoat buttons typical of a well-nourished man.

Fenzil falls into a brown study and sucks at his cigar as at an opium pipe. His shoulders sag; his head bows. He appears in danger of collapsing, like a cake disturbed in the oven.

"Doctor." I tug at his sleeve, and he awakes from his reverie and inflates once more to the full authority of a Union army captain and surgeon.

"Tell me about Mr. Poe." I have often been in thrall to his eerie tales, which the envious critic

Rufus Griswold claimed were written either by an opium eater or a sot. I doubt it's possible to compose so artfully when the mind is drugged or fuddled with drink.

"When I first set eyes on Poe, he'd come for a look at Dr. Mütter's curiosities. It was not until his second visit that we spoke. We found each other sympathetic, and for a time, I was his protégé." Fenzil pauses in his recollection to flick the lengthening ash from his cigar. "Once he took me to a hanging. Damned thing to take a green boy to see a man swing! Poe was like that; he enjoyed other people's discomfiture." So does his former protégé. "He relished human nature in extremis. By the end of that winter, I was glad to be rid of him, although, as I said, I still read his tales. I don't care for the poems—too jingly-jangly." Fenzil draws on his cigar, but the life of it—the ember— is spent. "Dr. Mütter made the greatest impression on me. He was a surgeon of enormous skill. He died in '59. I watched him correct one of nature's ghastly mistakes; he undid a poor fellow's deformity. You never saw such courage as that young man showed as Mütter cut and sewed his mouth without a drop of ether, which had not yet come into use, except among the Irish, who used it to circumvent their pledge to do without strong drink. Never once did the poor fellow cry out, though he sweated buckets."

I'm eager to hear more about Edgar Poe, but Fenzil is reluctant to go on.

"I've drained those days from my mind like a carbuncle," he says, pursing his lips. "It was a time in my life I've no wish to revisit."

An ambulance lumbers into the yard, bearing its dismal cargo. The horses are played out, poor beasts. Six hospital attendants take their time unloading the wagon of its wounded. They pack them off to the wards on stretchers, where they will worsen and die, get well and return to the battlefield, or be invalided home. Patients already in residence call them "veal."

"Which is the worse fate?" asks Fenzil. "To be shot through the vitals and die quickly or to hobble home on a Jewett's artificial leg?"

"In Concord, I'd have said that—hobble, crawl, or be carried—it's better to be alive than dead."

"And now?" There's that penetrating gaze of his again!

"I don't know."

"Therein lies wisdom," he says, pulling a face that could pass for a smile on a man who seems to wear a habitual frown.

"Forty ambulances arrived my first week here," I say in a tone that, try though I did, could not remain neutral, but must express rage that such a thing could be in the year 1863. (I admit to feeling prideful, too, that I have thus far stuck.)

"Fredericksburg and the Mud March were a bloody mangle! Abe Lincoln ought to have Burnside dragged out by his side-whiskers and shot!"

I decide that I don't dislike Edward Fenzil, although, as night closes on Georgetown, his presence is as warming as a cold stove. Something is missing in the man.

"Does Mrs. Ropes ever let you off the leash, Miss Alcott?"

"Sunday afternoons."

"The army does not indulge its nurses, then."

He has gotten my back up again. "We're not here to be indulged, Mr. Fenzil!"

"Of course not. I beg your pardon. I was only wondering if you could—on your half day—show me the sights of Washington City."

"I've seen no sights, except those that can be glimpsed during the carriage ride from the Baltimore and Ohio depot in Washington to Union Hospital in Georgetown."

"Then should we not see them together, Miss Alcott? On Sunday?"

Careful, Louisa! You've written about mesmerists with piercing eyes and can forecast a likely outcome to an invitation to "see the sights." Don't be ridiculous, Lu! Your imaginative faculty is inflamed. Your inner eye has a sty. Mr. Fenzil is neither Franz Anton Mesmer nor a Hindu Thuggee. His coat may be in need of brushing, but it does not reek of hashish. I see no danger in a Sunday-afternoon walk.

"I doubt there's time to see many," I reply, allowing myself to smile.

"Washington City is not so very large, surely."

"Larger than Timbuktu, whose streets, I understand, are cleaner."

It is his turn to smile, although the effect is peculiar. His mouth seems to lack suppleness. I'm reminded of someone attempting to walk after a lengthy convalescence. "I would like to visit the Naval Observatory before I leave," he says.

"You're leaving Washington?" I steady my voice, so as—so as to what, Lu?

"The day after our sightseeing, as it turns out."

How do you feel about that, Louisa?

Relieved, if I'm honest. Granted I write—or my nom de plume, A. M. Barnard, does—about romance. But I don't wish for one. Money, not a man, is my end and aim. The Pathetic Family is in perpetual debt, thanks to Father's improvidence, and I must rub-a-dub-dub to pay the butcher, baker, and candlestick maker. It falls to me alone to provide for Mother and Abby May. For all I care, Father can take a room in the madhouse and carry on his Conversations with the residents! I have an obligation to literature, though "Pauline's Peril and Punishment" squats at the foot of the mountain on whose summit Dickens, Thackeray, Trollope, Hawthorne, Eliot, and Waldo Emerson stand and gab. (God Almighty, I'm still waiting for *The Atlantic Monthly* to pay me my ten-dollar royalty for "Debbie's Debut"!)

Shall I be honest?

I don't care two straws if Debbie never makes her debut, except that I can't send another story till she's launched. Mr. Fields, editor of *The Atlantic Monthly*, tells me that war stories are what sells. I'll write "till from my bones my flesh be hacked," if only he'll take them, for money is the staff of life and without it one falls flat, no matter how much genius she may have packed in her portmanteau.

"Well, Miss Alcott?"

"I'd be delighted." Perhaps my writing will be galvanized by a mesmeric current passing from Poe to me through the medium of Edward Fenzil.

Stuff and nonsense, Miss Alcott!

I ARRANGED TO MEET EDWARD FENZIL at the Naval Observatory, certain that the matron would disapprove of one of her nurses being shown the town by an army surgeon, whose manners are likely to have been coarsened by overfamiliarity with gross matter. Like Superintendent Dix, Hannah Ropes believes that female nurses should be plain. My looking glass would say that I am otherwise, unless it flatters or I deceive myself. I suppose that I'm capable of self-deception, being of the imaginative sort. No, I don't believe that Edward—I'll call him by his Christian name, if only to myself—would have shown an interest if I were so *very* plain. My chestnut hair is luxuriant, my figure ample, my gaze, as has been noted, is full of meaning. What awful tripe, Louisa! Lizzie was the pretty Alcott girl; you, my dear, are large—a description complimentary to horses but not to young women, unless they're meant to pull a plow.

After listening to the chaplain fulminate against the secessionists and ask God to strike General Lee dead at His earliest convenience, I go to my room and get into my Concord clothes. I put on the earbobs given me by a giant of a New Hampshire man, who purloined them from a house in Fredericksburg. A rebel shell gave him his comeuppance and blew his leg to hell—or to high Heaven if the Almighty is a Unionist, as the chaplain avers. I squint at the gorgeous grapes of amethyst in a mirror sized to deliver us from vanity, being no larger than a muffin.

Leaving by the back door, with the stealth of a weasel slipping into a chicken house to suck eggs, I hurry along Twenty-ninth Street as fast as Sabbath decorum and my skirts allow. I take a Water Street horsecar to Rock Creek, cross the bridge, and board a second car heading to the two-story observatory in the Washington neighborhood known as Foggy Bottom. Like most of the city's other public buildings, the observatory is in the Greek Revival mode, though its stuccoed bricks are not so regal and serene as the Capitol's sandstone. As I step down from the car into E Street, the sky is lowering. I congratulate myself for having thought to bring an umbrella.

Edward is waiting, a cigar stuck between his

bearded lips. Why must men smoke a thing that smells no better than old mattress ticking smoldering on an ash heap? A Transcendentalist's parlor smells only of overheated brains and flammable passions of the purely intellectual type—or so I remember it. (In memory's backward view, Waldo and my foolish father wear togas, and dear, mischievous Henry capers like Pan playing the syrinx.)

"Good afternoon, Miss Alcott." Edward tips his army officer's hat.

"Mr. Fenzil." I nod my head, in lieu of dropping a curtsy, which none but Queen Victoria deserves and she only out of respect for George Eliot, who shares her natal year.

"Won't you call me Edward?"

"I can think of no reason why I should."

"In the spirit of democracy."

"Well, in the spirit of democracy, I will." So long as you don't quote Whitman to me.

We walk up a flight of granite steps and enter the observatory. The rooms are of little interest to me, but Edward finds the place fascinating. Walking amid glass cases, he admires the sextants, quadrants, chronometers, and other navigational instruments (so much cleaner than the surgical ones he wields), and peruses charts appertaining to the two firmaments in the story of creation. I recall the charts that Father drew when he was mad, showing the invisible forces governing the universe—from the rat in the wall to the queen in her palace.

"Being here, I'm reminded of my days as custodian of Dr. Mütter's collection," says Edward—a little wistfully, I think. "The jars always needed to be cleaned of smudges, and the exhibits dusted. I cataloged diseased organs, gallstones, skulls, bones, teeth, tiny pink fetuses floating in alcohol. The display cases were reliquaries of the malformed, the morbid, and the carious."

"It sounds like Barnum's American Museum."

"But with a serious purpose, Louisa."

I allow him the familiarity and would have given curiosity its head had a naval officer not shouted "Good day!" from a gallery beneath the observatory's high domed ceiling. As he comes down the spiral stairs, I notice his prosthetic leg.

Edward stands to attention and makes his salute, which the officer carelessly returns.

"We don't get many visitors." He shows me the courtesy of touching the brim of his hat. "Ma'am." He nods to Edward, whom he outranks. "I'm Lieutenant Commander Josiah Bostick." He points aloft. "Upstairs is my crow's nest and quarterdeck. He raps a knuckle on his artificial leg—first the leather thigh and then the wooden shin. "I took shrapnel at Hampton Roads, aboard the *Monitor*."

"The ironclad!" says Edward respectfully. "I read of her encounter with the *Virginia*."

"For three hours, we do-si-doed, wove the ring, boxed the gnat, and then we went to our separate corners and sulked. In any case, the navy gave me command of the observatory, where the only peril I face is falling down the stairs."

He sits in an upholstered chair. "Forgive me, miss, for being less than gallant."

"She nurses at Union Hospital," says Edward, as if a woman of my occupation would naturally countenance all lapses in etiquette.

I don't give a hangnail about etiquette, and nothing has been able to shock me since I nursed the Pathetic Family through cholera, smallpox, and the scarlet fever that carried off dear Lizzie, whose heart was racked by it. In her last days, I fed her opium, thinking all the while of De Quincey's *Confessions*. (A basket of Communion crackers chased with holy water could not have eased her pain.) In that dank, wretched house in Bedford Street, I heard my father ask his daughter as she drew near her end, "Have you some notions of your state after the change?" I thought I'd been transported into Poe's story of the "Strange Case of M. Valdemar," when the poor man is asked, "Can you explain to us what are your feelings or wishes now?"

"Ah, then you've seen us at our worst!" says Josiah Bostick, who can't read minds and does not know the thoughts that have been chasing one another through my brain.

"And best," I say, thinking of John Sulie, a most comely man. He bore his wounds and fate bravely, so much so that I cannot help but admire him. The surgeon gave me the task of telling John that his wound was a mortal one. He took the news without complaint. Neither by word nor by the mute appeal that eyes can make did he ask for my pity. *There* was a man I could have loved!

"I imagine so," says Bostick. "A man will either rise to glory or fall into disgrace, as his temperament and circumstances dictate. There's not much in the middle that I have seen." He regards Edward and says, "I seldom get an army man in here."

"I've always been interested in science and machinery."

"We had the first time ball in the country. It's been up on the roof since 1845. Charles Goodyear vulcanized it to Lieutenant Maury's specifications. Maury was superintendent of the Naval Observatory and head of the Depot of Charts and Instruments. They used to call him the 'Pathfinder of the Seas.' A Virginian, he went over to the rebels at the beginning of the war." Bostick straightens his leg and rubs the place where his stump frets against the leather thigh. "Excuse me, miss, but my missing leg does throb on occasion, since I've been beached."

"What is a time ball?" I'm not the least curious, but one must stick one's oar in now and then, or be thought of as a lump.

"Too bad you came today; Sunday is the only day we don't drop it."

"Drop what?" asks Edward, sensing my annoyance at Bostick's do-si-doing.

"Why, the time ball! It's a big rubber-coated ball painted gold that slowly slides down a pole on the roof. The instant it comes to rest marks the mean solar noon. Ships on the Potomac below us set their chronometers by it before putting out to sea, and the people in the city set their watches."

Bostick fiddles with his artificial leg. I suppose that if we weren't here, he'd take it off, as a man takes off a shoe that pinches.

"It's a shame Maury went over to the rebels. We lost plenty of naval and merchant ships after he invented his electric torpedo. He was a genius."

God save us from geniuses!

Bostick gets to his feet. "I've got some correspondence to see to. Why don't you go aloft and take a peek at the telescope? When John Quincy Adams was president, he liked to look at the stars through it. Now Mr. Lincoln does."

"Mr. Lincoln?" How wonderful to picture him bent over the eyepiece, as if searching for mankind's last hope!

"He'll sit up there half the night, wrapped in his old shawl. Mind the steps as you go."

Edward and I have begun to climb the spiral stairs when Bostick looks up from his desk. "Another interesting thing about Lieutenant Maury: In '51, he sent Herndon and Gibbon to map the valley of the Amazon. He believed that we could solve the slavery problem and appease the abolitionists if slave owners could be persuaded to move their negroes to Brazil. He was a man of vision."

Edward must sense my indignation, because he takes my arm and draws me up the stairs, my large feet shod in boots that once climbed Mount Monadnock.

"Miss Alcott, it serves no purpose to unlimber your gun."

"Maybe so, but I'd like to unlimber my umbrella on his thick skull!"

Edward disarms me of the means to do battery.

"He's well-meaning."

"That doesn't make him any less a fool."

"I see you don't suffer them gladly."

"Mr. Fenzil, I do not!"

"I shall do my best not to say anything foolish, Miss Alcott."

His gaze is impudent, and I return it in kind. "There isn't time for much foolishness, since you're leaving Washington tomorrow."

"Then we should encourage our serious selves. What do you think of the telescope, Miss Alcott? The barrel—what would you say? Two hands' breadth. We might see the famous goats and unicorns of the moon. Or the bat men, which spend the lunar days building pyramids sacred to the sun."

"Are you making fun of me?"

"Why yes, I am."

"I've no objection to being teased, so long as you do not flirt." I examine a much smaller telescope. "Which way is Concord?"

He turns the instrument to the northeast.

"What a lark it would be to watch Waldo shoveling his walk or my sister trudging down the pike in her gusset boots!"

"The Reverend Thomas Dick estimated the lunar population at four million two hundred thousand—he did not say 'souls.' The reverend was much admired by the Sage of Concord."

"I doubt Mr. Emerson would've been taken in! I shall ask him about it when I return to Concord." Edward makes the male gesture of dismissal I find so infuriating. "Mr. Fenzil, I hate being shrugged at!"

He points the telescope at me.

"What do you see?" I ask.

"Your heart."

"Does it appear to be in good health?"

"It's decorated with a black crepe ribbon."

"Nonsense!" Annoyed, I swivel the instrument so that I may regard him.

"What do you see, Louisa?" he asks a trifle solemnly.

"A frivolous nature."

"If only it were true," he responds with a ruefulness that makes me tremble.

He swings the telescope around and aims it at my bonnet, as a captain of artillery would a howitzer loaded with a twenty-four-pound shell. For a second time, I tremble.

"While I was at Jefferson Medical College, Dr. Mütter became curious to understand how carrier pigeons are able to find their way home over great distances—as far as six hundred miles across mountains and through storms. He removed scores of their tiny brains and studied them under the microscope, hunting for a faculty he never found."

"And were you to scoop out mine, what would you find?" I'm not sure that I want to hear his answer.

"An intelligent mind, not much given to flights of fancy."

"I'm pleased to hear it, Mr. Fenzil!" If only you knew the wayward imagination of A. M. Barnard!

He turns an iron wheel, and a section of the observatory dome slides back to reveal the sky, which has blackened since our arrival. He climbs a ladder, stands in the opening, and loses his hat to a blast of icy rain. Shaking his fist at it, he reminds me of Captain Ahab in the shrouds of the *Pequod,* cursing both God and Leviathan. The thought crosses my mind that Edward is, at once, a romantic figure and a tragic one. I shudder for a reason other than the cold draught striking my own face. I tug at his trouser leg, urging him to come inside. As he does, I crank the roof hatch shut.

As a breeze might turn a page of a book I'm reading, so that I find myself in the midst of a new scene, the memory of Hawthorne's "sky parlor" has been brought to mind—the room at the top of the three-story tower that he had built for his Concord house. By that time, that grim and silent man had written *The Scarlet Letter, The House of the Seven Gables,* and *The Blithedale Romance* and freed Sophia and himself from poverty. I pray to the god of scribblers that my novel *Moods* will do as much for Marmee, May, and me. Hawthorne's house had once belonged to the hapless Alcotts—another gift bestowed on them by saintly Mr. Emerson.

I owe a good deal also to my mother, Marmee, though I'm glad to be living apart from her crack-brained husband. Were it not for this war, I'd be in Concord—an industrious daughter, on equal terms with Attic philosophers and a manure spreader. How happy I am to have escaped the poorhouse, workhouse, and madhouse that were the Alcotts' home! At thirty, I look back on a bewildering succession of "residences" (Orchard House, the twenty-ninth), as the peripatetic family moved from pillar to post. Wherever we went, so did the nicheless bust of Socrates—the only item from Father's Temple School not seized by his creditors after his noble experiment in education failed. We women dressed like beggars. We were considered "dreadful wild people"—the object of jeers, rude stares, mortifying pity, and supercilious glances, a target of insults and stones hurled by small boys. But always Waldo Emerson stood by, prepared to lift us from the squalor brought about by Father's airy idleness. When I was aware enough to know how things stood, I burned with shame to be a member of such a feckless tribe. I would have taken arms against that sea of troubles, which threatened the balance of Prince Hamlet's mind, were it not for Mr. Emerson and my mother and sisters.

"Miss Alcott, I fear the Last Judgment has arrived," says Edward, setting his disordered hair to rights as the outer darkness closes round about us.

"I'm ready for it, Mr. Fenzil."

"I don't doubt it."

When we lived in Boston, Marmee was a city missionary to the poor and perishing while the Alcotts were poor and perishing and Father was having Conversations! In the summer of 1851, he had the gall to *proclaim* his love for Ednah Dow Littlehale, a twenty-seven-year-old devotee. (Father's spark may be hot and bright, but it produces nothing but a squib.) Mother let things run their course—that is her way with him. Had I been she, after enduring poverty, the humiliation at Fruitlands, and Miss Littlehale, in addition to the domestic tyranny of Mr. Lane, who nearly persuaded Father to run away with *him,* I'd have done to Bronson, with his walking stick, what the venal knights did to Edward II in his privy! "What use is Lieutenant Maury's time ball in a world whose people are at odds?" I ask Edward. "What earthly good to know the time of day when everyone disagrees?"

He raises my furled umbrella above his head. "Do you recall these lines by Poe? 'I took from their sconces two flambeaux, and giving one to Fortunato, bowed him through several suites of rooms to the archway that led into the vaults. I passed down a long and winding staircase, requesting him to be cautious as he followed.'"

"'The Cask of Amontillado.'"

"Just so," says Edward. "Allow me to go first, Louisa."

I let him lead the way. Not until women shed their skirts in favor of bloomers will we be equal to the negotiation of spiral stairs.

MY WET CLOTHES ARE PINNED to a line above the stove in the attic bedroom that I share with Nurse Crawford, who is on night duty. I arrived at Union Hospital soaked to the skin by the walk from the car stop at Twenty-ninth and Water. Matron was preoccupied by a hysterical novice. As I stole upstairs, Lucy Higgs told me that the new girl's hooped skirt had caught on the sutures of one of the men as he lay in his cot, and having become unstitched, he bled to death. Hoops and crinolines are forbidden in the wards. Why the new nurse disobeyed is a puzzle, unless she had come to Washington in the hope of leaving with a husband. Tomorrow will provide the answer; the other nurses will be buzzing with the story. I pity the girl, who will lose her place but never the memory of what happened here.

As the rain hissed beyond the observatory portico, Edward insisted on finding a hackney cab to take me back to the hospital. No sooner had he gone in search of one than I dashed into the wet night, as impulsively as a silly Jane Austen heroine who sets off on a walk across the grassy downs, only to be caught in a downpour and punished for her impetuosity by a dreadful cold or a sprained foot. Lord knows what Edward must have thought, coming back with the cab, to find me gone! Well, he's off to war tomorrow. I doubt our paths shall cross again, unless it be in a fictional setting—Naples or the Azores, where we shall walk the well-worn paths of sentimental fiction. As for myself, I don't care a button if I die a spinster! Jane Austen was one, George Eliot another. The Brontë sisters required no husbands to fulfill them. "I am no bird; and no net ensnares me. I am a free human being with an independent will." So wrote Charlotte, or else it was Emily. Spinsterhood may agree with me so long as I don't end up like Miss Havisham, who was a man's creation—which is to say, his creature.

> . . . she had secluded herself from a thou-
> sand natural and healing influences; that,

> her mind, brooding solitary, had grown
> diseased, as all minds do and must and
> will that reverse the appointed order of
> their Maker . . .

(God, too, is said to be a man, as men never tire of telling us to keep us underfoot.)

The thought of the young Edward Fenzil wiping the smudges from a glass jar containing Miss Havisham's pickled brain pops into my head, and I shake it off as I would a fly that had settled on my nose.

What will become of the hapless nurse who killed a man with her skirts? A sad business. She's a pretty thing. I expect she'll marry and fret when her man goes off to war. What happens to women whose men never come home? Do they needlepoint sentimental mottoes on cambric with which to decorate their purgatory? I'd rather write about widows than be one. How lucky that Edward has left me for the glories of the battlefield! I pray to the god of the Unitarians to spare him. I pray to the gods of the Baptists, the Methodists, the Catholics, the Hebrews, and the Hindus for good measure—nor do I neglect Him of the Transcendentalists, whose initials are R.W.E. I also pray that my clothes will dry by morning, or the matron will have something astringent to say that will make my mouth pucker.

Since I'm not likely to fall asleep tonight—I feel restless and ill at ease—I'll write to Mother.

I get paper and pen, but before I've even begun,

I stop, wondering what I ought to write. Dear Marmee, an officer, who is not quite a gentleman, showed me the Naval Observatory this afternoon. I returned to my little roach-ridden room drenched and liable to catch cold, if not my death. He leaves tomorrow for Virginia, and good riddance. I could not bear a man with dirty nails.

If I were to marry, Mother would have a conniption fit. Or would she? Has she never imagined me as a bride? Maybe she knows I'm not cut out of the stuff wives are made of. I'll write her some other day, when my head is clear. And I'll keep Mr. Fenzil to myself—not even my journal shall know of him. For now, I'll cork up my feelings.

"MISS ALCOTT!"

Matron Ropes has found me in the linen closet, where I'm hiding in case one of her spies has informed her of my Sunday-afternoon dalliance, which is the word she would doubtless use to describe my sally into Washington on the arm of a man. I'm prepared to protest that I did not sally, dally, or take anybody's arm. It seems, however, that she hasn't come to chastise me.

"Mr. Gardner of Mathew Brady's photographic establishment is coming this afternoon to take a picture of the ward. The secretary of war asked that we matrons make available several of our prepossessing nurses for Mr. Gardner's camera. I believe his exact words to Superintendent Bliss, who conveyed them without varnish to Superintendent Dix, were, 'I don't care to see any Temperance battleaxes hovering over the wounded.' You can appreciate Miss Dix's emotions—and mine—but we must swallow our indignation for the cause."

I nearly smile to hear myself called "prepossessing," but I know that smiles are frowned upon unless they be the beatific sort seen on the faces of the chaplain and the devoutly Christian soldiers at the moment they expire. "I'll do what I can to be useful, Matron," I say like a frantic husband asked to boil water by a midwife.

Matron nods and leaves me to count the half shirts and the linens.

Why didn't Edward ask for my photograph or a favor such as women are apt to bestow on men going to war? He might have done so in the cab, but like a flibbertigibbet, I ran away! Louisa, you mustn't soften; your heart must be a cash box until the Alcott family is no longer in arrears! Remember Mr. Fenzil's cigar-stained teeth, ragged nails, and the wild look that would sometimes overtake him. I doubt much good will come to the woman who consents to be his wife. You're well and safely out of *that*.

And what, pray tell, was "that"?

Three hours spent with a man who never spoke a fond syllable, much less breathed a sigh of regret at his imminent departure! Your imagination is diseased, Louisa; you ought to have it out before you take to swooning and blushing and such arts of the weaker sex, of which you are not one! Romance is not for you, my dear, except for that which is carried on inside the covers of a novelette.

I hurry upstairs to put a ribbon in my hair. "Your hair is your best feature, Lu," Mother always says. I admire its gloss and thickness in the modest mirror on the wall. God will forgive us our little vanities. I look out the window at a boat ferrying colored troopers to Mason's Island. The glass panes are imperfect, and I see things imperfectly. From my window at Orchard House, I can see Walden Pond shimmering in the distance above the elm trees. How sad that my Henry's gone! How he used to make me laugh! He was a divine fool as much as a philosopher. May they not be one and the same? Mr. Emerson never makes me laugh, although I adore him, and blush to remember how I used to walk outside his house at all hours. What must Lidian have thought of me? Waldo had his female devotees, and, perhaps, she, too, let things peter out.

Having returned to the "ballroom," which the largest ward was in gayer times, I change a dressing for a young man whose larynx was nicked by musket shot during the crossing of the Rappahannock. He fingers the wound curiously, as if it belonged to somebody else. He seems not to mind that he won't be able to speak again. Maybe he's relieved; speech can be a burden, and most of what gets said is a waste of breath.

The nurses are putting clean bandages on the wounded men and sheets on the beds in advance of Mr. Gardner and his camera. The porters empty chamber pots and align pairs of boots, though some of their owners may henceforth need only one of them, or none. Matron looks on disapprovingly at the hurly-burly—a fitting name for this hectic scrimmage that may send someone prematurely to the undiscovered country, whose anteroom is the dead house in our cellar.

Last night as I sat by the stove in my chemise, it came to me that stories can be written about my experiences at Union Hospital, to satisfy Mr. Field and his bloodthirsty readers. I can imagine a book of them entitled *In the Dead House*. No, with such a ghoulish title, it could be mistaken for a recently discovered work of Poe's. The niter-encrusted walls of Union Hospital resemble his description of the damp catacombs belonging to the Montresors. It's no wonder so many of our sick and wounded die of fever and pneumonia! The walls ought to be cleaned with bread, but not even the twenty brick ovens in the Capitol Building's cellar, where the army bakers make their "worm castles," could supply enough loaves to rid our peeling walls of grime.

The big bug of publishing, James T. Field, would

never dare doubt my qualifications if I were to write about a long-legged hobbledehoy who leaves home to nurse the wounded. I'll call her Tribulation Periwinkle, a name with a Dickensian aroma, who goes to Hurly-burly House to be of use. Might not a book of sketches on events in which I'm certain to be entangled admit me to the club of serious authors? Even if posthumously published, such a book would be a moneymaker for poor, put-upon, long-suffering Marmee, who, I've promised, will one day reside in "a chamber whose name is Peace." And by that, I didn't mean her coffin!

Gardner and his assistant arrive. Lu, you mustn't act undignified in front of the matron. Think how Edward would scowl to see you mince about like a silly woman trying on a hat. Damn Mr. Fenzil! I'll purge myself of him if it takes a quart of castor oil. I will think of the Transcendentalists instead. They stand on their dignity and sit on it, as well. All but Henry, whose pants were patched. Louisa, one doesn't say *pants* in mixed company. They were patched all the same.

"Ladies, stand by the beds!" says Gardner brusquely, as you would expect of a man who photographs corpses, whose ears are deaf to rude commands.

Matron claps her hands. "Nurses, take your places!"

We pass nervously amid our wounded, each of

us stealing an appraising glance at the others of the "pretty" sorority, in the hope of finding fault. I can honestly say that I don't suffer by comparison. Of the six of us, only Fanny Warren, whose hair is flaxen and complexion fair, is handsomer than I (though I tend toward the monumental).

Gardner comes out from the dark cloth behind the tripod camera and instructs his assistant in how we nurses ought to be positioned. He does the master's bidding, moving each of us slightly or entirely, to best effect. I'm directed to leave the mute soldier to himself and stand in the foreground. Matron, looking fierce, wheels an amputee toward me. Gardner comes from behind his camera and, taking me by the wrist, arranges the tableau. I'm shocked by his rough manner and am about to protest, when the matron rebukes him.

"Mr. Gardner, do not manhandle the nurses!" Her tone is imperious, and she jumps up yards in my esteem.

Gardner glares and shrugs. I've said before how I hate that rudely dismissive gesture. He returns to the camera, disappears underneath the drape, and waves his hand at me. I step back. He says something to the assistant, who asks if I would kindly take another step backward. I do, and a beam of light falls on my face from a skylight. He returns to Gardner, receives additional instructions, and moves the wheelchair to the left. The amputee is treated like meat in a butcher's

shop window. (His stump, which was hurriedly fashioned, resembles a ruddy ham instead of the tidier
"fish mouth.") Gardner asks Nurse Crane if she will
please not smile. The assistant puts the glass negative
in the camera and says, "Ready."

Gardner uncovers the lens, counts, and covers it.

"Thank you, ladies," says the assistant as he folds
the tripod and, with Gardner, departs for the ward
where the worst casualties are kept. I don't imagine
Secretary of War Stanton will allow their images to
be shown. Aghast, even the most zealous abolitionists might demand an end to the fighting—emancipation be damned! The mistreated Irish (called "green
niggers" by some) already resent having to fight for
the negroes and the rich.

Matron claps her hands. "The beauty pageant is
over!"

I push the dismembered soldier to his customary
place by the window.

"How come I lost my leg, and not them?" he
asks, pointing to soldiers marching down M Street.
Unable to think of a comforting reply, I say nothing.
Lucy Higgs, passing with a bundle of sheets in her
arms, reproves him. "Why do you think He gives
us two legs, Corporal Downs, only to take one of
them away?"

"So we can hop without getting all tanglefooted
up, Miss Lucy!"

They laugh, like two people who never tire of the same joke.

"I'd sure admire a taste of tanglefoot," he says slyly.

"You get well, and I'll bring you a bottle," she says, patting him on the shoulder. She walks away, carrying the sheets in her arms, and I'm struck by the contrast of the white linen against her black skin.

When I see her later, I ask about Corporal Downs.

"He likes to grouse, but he don't mean it. He's a religious man and knows he can lean on the Lord without being scared of falling."

"I'd sooner put my trust in Mr. Jewett's leg."

"You a religious woman, Miss Alcott?"

"Not so you'd notice."

"Why don't you come Sunday and listen to the preacher and eat supper with us after?" She studies my face a moment. "Unless you don't feel comfortable in a room full of darkies." Her eyes are lively, either with curiosity or malice. I'd guess it is the former.

"I'll have you know, Miss Higgs, that I am an abolitionist!" I declare, bristling with the self-righteousness of a teetotaler caught spiking her lemonade with gin. "My father is a Concord station-master on the Underground Railroad. My mother hid a runaway in her oven. I shared my room with John Brown's daughters, after the army hanged him."

Lucy Higgs laughs merrily. "Miss Alcott, you

don't need to show me your petticoat! And I sure hope the oven wasn't lit."

I feel my face coloring.

"Come along with me Sunday, Miss Alcott. We're a lot perkier than the pitiful souls squirming in their chairs while Reverend Miller puts the Lord to sleep. Come and listen to John Holmes preach."

To the squalling of a badly played melodeon, no doubt.

THE ESTERBROOK PEN THAT Julian Hawthorne bought for me in Boston as I prepared to leave for Washington broke under the strain of furious composition.

Wishful thinking, Miss Alcott! You've written precious little since arriving at Union Hospital, except letters on behalf of the wounded and, harder, the deceased. The truth of the matter is the nib broke as I tried to dig a deathwatch beetle from the wall.

My work done for the day, I visit a stationer's shop near the War Department to purchase a pen, though not an Esterbrook, whose cost exceeds my means. I choose instead one of Felt's steel pens, as well as a bottle of ink and a new journal to fill. I intend to write copiously about my days and nights at Hurly-burly House. I shall retire A. M. Barnard, whom the reading public believes to be a man. I've grown too ambitious to see my pages published under any other name but Louisa May Alcott. To hell with the stuffy sobersides of Concord, who don't care to have a blood and thunder authoress in their midst! I will give them the bitter pill of truth to swallow.

"We have the new German inks," says the shopkeeper, who has been eyeing my ample bosom and chestnut-colored hair. "The ladies like to pen their billets-doux in mauve or peacock blue. Lovely colors for a lovely young woman."

Billets-doux! Mauve ink! I cast a baleful black-eyed gaze on him in the hope of scorching him or turning him to stone—a block of Quincy granite, a monument to the arrogance of his sex.

"Black ink, if you please," I say severely.

"As madam wishes." He grotesquely parodies a courtly bow.

The insect has succeeded in making me furious.

"I want something to read," I say, dissembling my contempt. "What do you suggest?"

"I have several titles by Maria Susanna Cummins. *Mabel Vaughn* is a great favorite with the ladies," he simpers.

"Do you have Mr. Whitman's *Leaves of Grass*?" I don't know what possessed me to ask, except perversity and the desire to watch the smug fool squirm in embarrassment or rise up on his dandy's heels in indignation. Either one would make a pleasing sight. (To see him fall down dead of apoplexy would be even more delightful.)

He sniffs like a man who has taken too much snuff. "Nutley and Murdock does not stock immoral books."

I pretend to be appalled by the opinion of Messrs. Nutley and Murdock in the matter of serious literature. "I've heard that the book has been praised by the greatest philosopher of our time!"

"And who might that be?"

"Why, Ralph Waldo Emerson! Need you ask?"

"Neither Mr. Nutley nor Mr. Murdock has any use for atheists. Nor do I. Your ideas are unwholesome!"

Hastily and haphazardly, he wraps my purchases in brown paper and string. Sternly, he tells me the sum owed, as if he were levying a fine for a gross indecency. The mealworm!

"In future, 'madam,' I suggest you patronize some other shop. Nutley and Murdock does not need nor esteem your custom."

I give what is for every puffed-up shop clerk the coup de grâce: "Little man, your shelves need dusting."

I leave not with a flounce of skirts but with a sweep of my cape across my shoulder, like Judith after beheading Holofernes.

"They ought to burn all such books!" he shouts from the door, which I haven't bothered to close behind me.

"Why stop at books?" I retort, my hands defiantly on my hips, which Concord's Dr. Bartlett complimented as ideal for childbearing. "Why not burn their authors at the stake?"

"I'd strike the match myself!" he shrieks, and is immediately abashed to find himself the center of attention on the bustling street. He hurries inside his shop and closes the door—too fiercely, for the window shivers and glass shards make their pleasant music on the pavement.

Delighted with myself, I gloat. "That was an amusing interlude, Louisa!" I don't give a hang who hears me!

Parcel in hand, I bend my steps toward the Georgetown bridge, recalling how attentively Julian had squired me around Boston as I made my final preparations to leave for Washington. He's a dear boy and quite smitten by May. What would you do, Louisa, if he were not sixteen, but something nearer your own thirty years? Like the temptress in a shocker, would you practice your wiles and steal him from your sister?

Pshaw, I have no wiles and am badly suited to the role of temptress! I don't want to be Nathaniel Hawthorne's daughter-in-law any more than I want to be known as Bronson Alcott's daughter. *I want to be I*—a tautological statement, but true, notwithstanding. I have no desire to end up like Maria in Mary Wollstonecraft's *The Wrongs of Woman*, who claims, "Marriage had bastilled me for life." I do so admire the damned clever way Wollstonecraft put it!

Hungry, I step inside a lunchroom on Water Street, near the river. Someone has left a copy of Whitman's old rag the *Brooklyn Daily Eagle*—a drummer, perhaps, having stopped to rest his feet and a valise packed with handkerchiefs or stove lids on the floor. My eyes fall on the front page, where an item in the "Foreign News and Gossip" column is circled in pencil:

> The office of the public executioner at Graze, in Austria, having become vacant, a considerable number of candidates presented themselves. A man has been chosen who proved that he had already dispatched into the other world, by the aid of the cord, not less than 135 criminals.

I don't have an inkling where Graze may be on the map of Europe, but reading the account (no more than an aside to the war news and lists of casualties), I'm moved, strangely. The cord, I think, disquiets me. That such a homely thing, used to do up a parcel, should have undone so many is poignant. Life must be sinister in Graze. In America, we dispatch the condemned with good Kentucky hemp or a firing squad. I prefer death by rope or bullet than by a fatal cord. How is it done? Does the executioner stand behind or before the "raw material" of his art? If the latter, I can imagine his determined mouth, flaring nostrils, popping eyes, and acrid breath as he twists the instrument by which he has unhoused 135 souls. To look at life for the last time and see *him*! To picture that man's face for eternity—surely it is punishment enough for the condemned of Graze! I order a cup of "rio," as the soldiers call coffee. When I taste it, my palate is excited by the pleasantly bitter memory of morning coffee drunk at the oilcloth-covered kitchen table with my mother and sisters—so unlike the puny facsimile boiled up in the hospital kitchen and served by Isaac, the negro porter, whose surname none has ever thought to ask.

"We've mince pie today," says a fat man dressed in an apron. The apron looks as though it had done duty in a surgery.

"I'm a vegetarian and don't eat mincemeat. Have you a cobbler? My shoes need soling."

He opens his mouth, doubtless to curse all smart alecks, but decides to bring me a piece of apple pie instead. I eat nearly all of it, remembering to "save a crumb for the Devil," as madwoman Nancy Barron used to say, admonishing Concord's children.

Outside on the pavement, I study the sky for portents. I see no "disasters in the sun" to send me hurrying back to the dead house before my time is up.

Where to now, Louisa?

To the Smithsonian to see James Audubon's rapture of birds!

I WALK THROUGH THE APPARATUS ROOM, where
Dr. Hare's electrical machine is on view. A few gentlemen in tailcoats and beaver hats are pontificating
before the vast complication, while their lady companions hide their boredom. One yawns behind a
pamphlet; another fidgets with her glove; an elderly
dame in a crinoline cage fingers a wen on her neck
as her milky eyes glaze.

By such an apparatus as Dr. Hare's, ironclads
will fly and rain Maury's electric torpedoes on foreign capitals like Havana, Manila, and Panama City.
America's appetite will grow ever larger, till it swallows whole nations and—leaving the table without
a crumb for the Devil—belches in satiety, which
will soon need to be appeased. (What of Graze? Is
it worth stealing from the Austrians? And of what
interest can its newly appointed executioner be to
someone stopping in a Georgetown eatery?)

I've come to the "Castle," as the turreted redbrick
Smithsonian is known, to see James Audubon's gorgeous birds. I can think of little more soothing to the
nerves than to stand awhile in admiration of nature's
artistry and Mr. Audubon's own. You need to wal-
low in color, Louisa, before the gray of the streets,
the bedsheets and pillowcases, the handkerchiefs and
bandages, the winter sky and leaden rivers, the sick
faces, and your nurse's uniform seeps into your disposition. It won't do to go frowning among the men.
They cotton to your genial ways, unlike those of some

other nurses—efficient and glum. Just once I'd like to unpin my hair and shake out my chestnut curls for the boys! The sight would surely get them dancing or hopping, as fate—incorporated in the graybacks and the U.S. Army surgeons—has decreed.

I recall the afternoon I pinned up my hair underneath one of Father's hats and dressed up in his clothes to get Julian Hawthorne's goat. He was standing in the yard, moonstruck by my pretty sister May. I swaggered up to her, put my arm around her waist, and kissed her lightly on the lips. With the indignation of his fourteen years, Julian struck me on the shoulder, as if I had been Ganymede instead of Rosalind, and Concord the forest of Arden. In response, I twisted the end of my dandy's mustache and sneered at him with so beautiful an insolence that I do believe he would have brained me with the garden rake had I not torn off my false whiskers. How splendid it would be to enact that little comedy here at Union Hospital, with Fanny as ingénue and me reprising my role as Simon Legree! It would do the patients' costive hearts a world of good—those, that is, we don't kill outright with belly laughs. The young private Arnold Moore would have made a fine Julian had amputation and sepsis not cut short his stage career.

I leave the Apparatus Room, fragrant with machine oil, violet drops, and peach pomade, for an outlandishly painted aviary. The white-feathered ptarmigan, pale pink avocet, orange-and-green

Florida cormorant, Arkansas flycatcher thatched with a red toupee, coppery bay-breasted warbler, black-backed gull showing an obscenely colored tongue, Bonaparte flycatcher sporting Burnside whiskers, green-ringed Carolina parrot looking piratical with a russet eye patch, scarlet ibis with a piercing gaze, scandalously pink flamingo, violet-and-bronze passenger pigeon, which men love to slaughter by the millions—all these irradiate the inmost self. By his skillful hand, the late Audubon called into being another order of creation. To stand before it is to be vexed with God for having made the northern parts of *His* creation drab, as though He hadn't paint to spare for the country of the Puritans.

You must get thee to Florida, Lu, when it's safe to travel. And may the stern judge of souls strike down any man, Union or Confederate, who brings fire to its meadows, woods, and mangrove swamps, as Jackson, Armistead, and Worth did to the homeland of the Seminoles! (We don't wish the red man dead, only removed to the minor hell that is Oklahoma Territory.)

"I wish you were here to see *this*!" I whisper to dearly departed Henry Thoreau, whom I loved as a girl, when I lived, together with the other Alcotts, in Edmund Hosmer's cottage, close to Walden Pond. (Or would you protest against a showy nature, as if it were a gaudy Paris gown, when a plain New England wren is finery enough? I can hear you say, "How many snowy egrets does it take to trim a lady's hat?" How you delighted in contrariety, my friend!)

I leave the Castle, prepared to concede that Earth may need Walt Whitman and his poetry to catalog its parts before they vanish, as did Eden, into the void of lost paradises (or succumb to a brutish nature, to speak like a Darwinian). Already Earth has lost its Guadeloupe parakeet and Mauritius owl. Who mourns for them other than the wind in the trees after the sun goes down? And will it always, I wonder, rise again—that sun—or one day cease?

On the bridge across Rock Creek, I peer over the railing at the livid water. As a tarnished mirror murders the faces that look to it for confirmation of their comeliness, or plainness, or the very existence of their owners, I see nothing of myself, the darkening sky that frames me, or so much as an inch below the steely surface of the water. The icy skin conceals the body's depths.

MR. OLSON WAS SCALDED when a laundry tub filled with boiling water and lye upset in the hospital yard. He threw himself into the snow where it had been piled to clear the way to the necessary house, which the nurses call the "shithouse." (No longer shocked by the sight of a man's entrails, we can scarcely be embarrassed by the common word for their contents.)

Two porters carried Mr. Olson into the ward

and laid him on a bed. When Fanny Warren tried to take off his shirt, the boiled skin came away. How the poor man howled! The attendants referred to him as "Mr. Lobster" until his death this morning. I saw no one cry. The ember at the human core is soon quenched. We care, our sympathies are intact, but the raw wound within the heart that burns at the touch of sorrow will shortly crust over with the sugar of habit. I hid in the linen cupboard and wept, not because I'm more compassionate than the others but because I have been in the wards only three weeks and already can foresee my loss of innocence. (If it were only a public shaming, such as befell Hester Prynne, I could endure it. But what forgiveness can there be when there is none to forgive us, what atonement for the guilt-ridden who has committed no sin? Better to be put into the stocks for all to see than to suffer the heart to grow callous. Better the stoning by the righteous mob than the stoning one gives herself for no other reason than she was taught to believe in her sinful nature.)

I accompany Mr. Olson to the dead house. There he will wait for his mother to arrange his burial. Those with none to claim them are laid to rest (what a pretty expression!) in the burial ground near the poorhouse and the asylum.

Like the genteel words I used to speak on the church porch or at the lyceum, wearing my bonnet and furbelows, the soul is of no use to me. Like books on etiquette or articles of faith, it is meaning-less now that the social contract has been ripped to shreds. None of the old consolations consoles me. Even Walt Whitman's idea of death and afterlife is as outmoded as that of Plato or Plotinus, Jonathan Edwards or Mr. Emerson. The body is an untenanted house no grander than a hovel, howsoever we conceal it beneath fancy Boston wallpaper. Already I've begun to lose my certainty as my hands root inside men's clay—no, Louisa! To say "clay" is to speak in an archaic style unsuitable to the age. In their gizzards and guts—in the dirt of them. There is a virginity of more consequence than what is signified by an intact hymen, and I expect to return to Concord without it.

ON SUNDAY, I GO TO CHURCH with Lucy Higgs. Because her means are slender, we walk instead of taking a car. The few negroes I've become acquainted with in Georgetown toil twelve-hour days without complaint or salary. To be allowed to work to ensure their own emancipation is thought to be adequate recompense. Careful of Lucy's pride, evident in the way she holds herself, I don't offer to pay her fare, although I would prefer to sit in a horsecar and rest my swollen legs.

Outside the Willard Hotel, onlookers crowd Pennsylvania Avenue to cheer soldiers of the Fourteenth Brooklyn Regiment—bayonets and gold

buttons dull beneath the overcast sky—as they herd
several hundred Union army deserters toward the
Old Capitol Prison. Conspicuous among the specta-
tors, Walt Whitman watches the sullen formation of
defeated men and doubtless finds the scene curious.
The deserters look like dilapidated fence pickets—
cockeyed and shoddy—in contrast to the Union soldiers smartly marching in their red trousers. Farther
down Pennsylvania Avenue, the Statue of Freedom
lies in the snow beside the Capitol, waiting to ascend
the unfinished cast-iron dome. I prefer the original
design, in which she wears a wreath of wheat and lau-
rel. This bronze Minerva capped with a crested helmet and leaning on a sword was the choice of former
Secretary of War Jefferson Davis. I don't care, either,
for the gargantuan George Washington astride
his bronze horse on the Capitol Mall; the German
sculptor made him look fierce and Napoleonic. The
mall would have been better served by the alder trees
that grew there before the city's architect, L'Enfant,
declared old Jenkins' Hill to be "a pedestal waiting
for a monument." How men love to put up monu-
ments to themselves! They exercise their egos, as if
they were horses preparing for the Grand National.

At the Charles Hotel, Lucy and I turn onto
West Second and follow a creek till we come to a
frame house with peeling paint, a rugged cross on
the porch roof, and a hand-lettered sign proclaiming THE AFRICAN METHODIST EPISCOPAL CHURCH OF

WASHINGTON. The windows are open to the cold air. Singing of a kind not heard in New England churches pours out in ecstatic gusts:

> Take up thy cross, nor heed the shame;
>> Nor let thy foolish pride rebel;
> Thy Lord for thee the cross endured,
>> To save thy soul from death and hell.

Lucy steers me onto the porch. She shoulders open the door, which creaks like the bones of some old sinner rising from the grave to hear his doom pronounced. We enter in time for her to add a dusky voice to the final lines of the hymn:

> Nor think till death to lay it down;
>> For only those who bear the cross
> May hope to wear the glorious crown.

We sit in the back. The stove is unlit; its heat would be superfluous to the fervor of fifty people of all ages jammed into the room. I watch them as the preacher begins to speak. He talks of the Lord, as though He were an elderly uncle whose house they'd be visiting by and by, or the man they call "Father Abraham." Ever since Lincoln signed the Emancipation Proclamation two weeks ago, the love they bear him could not be greater if he had knelt before each person of the negro race and personally struck off his chains.

Lucy Higgs used to be a slave in Grays Creek,

Tennessee. In June, she got away from her master and the slave catchers' dogs to the Union lines, and then, after wading across the Potomac at low water, arrived in Georgetown. Having nursed her master in his venereal disease and her mistress in childbirth and lung fever, Lucy was deemed experienced in the body's catastrophes and put to work at Union Hospital. As a colored sister, she receives no pay.

The preacher has gotten louder and more urgent. He no longer coddles and consoles; he exhorts the ecstatic congregation. He shakes the dusky rafters with his thunder. He presses the demands of Almighty God upon his people. He speaks like a prophet foreseeing ruin. The people answer with clapped hands, hallelujahs, and moans, as though possessed by the Spirit, which the Reverend John Holmes is invoking in the decrepit house of God behind the Baltimore Railroad depot.

"We are in a dark time of the year, when the sun is feeble, and we hunger for green things of the land and of the spirit. Preacher John, you ask, why do the sun shine on white folks when my people are made to stand in the shade?"

"Why, Lord?" asks the congregation in a single voice, whose tone is one of bafflement and hurt.

"What I care about the sun?" replies John Holmes scornfully. "The day comes on when the sun will be called from his racetrack, and his light squinted out forever."

"Dark day a-coming to us all!"

"The moon shall turn to blood, and the earth be consumed with fire."

"Blood moon, world all burned up!"

"Let the moon and the earth go; that won't scare me."

"Why ain't you scared, Preacher John?"

"Because the Word of the Lord shall endure forever, and on that Solid Rock we stand and shall not be moved."

The entire congregation stands and shouts, "Oh, Lord, we shall not be moved!"

"People say the sun don't move a peg. Well, it looks to me he moves around mighty brisk and is ready to go any way that the Lord orders him to go."

"That's so! All power unto the Lord!"

"He can put old sun in his pocket like a gold watch," says Holmes. "He can set the time a-running backwards or forwards. He can tell the sun to come up over the meanest crib. And He can blow it out like a candle on the roof of a fine mansion!"

"You right, He can!"

"With the sun's rays, He can call forth the fruit of the land. He can make it shine always and forevermore on negroes same as on any other folks. I put myself into the hands of the Lord! I put my two hands in His and will be upheld! Amen."

"Into the Lord's hands! Amen!"

We are on our feet and shouting "Amen!" and

"Hallelujah!" I'm embraced; my cheek is kissed. I'm engulfed by the warm risen bread of fellowship. Raucously, we sing:

> Joshua fit de battle ob Jerico, Jerico,
>   Jerico
> Joshua fit de battle ob Jerico
> An' de walls come tumblin' down.

The roughly plastered walls, plain ceiling, unvarnished floors, mismatched chairs, and an altar hammered together out of old boards and adorned with a cloth stitched in bright threads no longer seem poor. As the voices are raised in rapture, the room is transformed, like the faces of the congregants made glorious by God's unseen presence. I think that this rude church is grand enough to entertain the Father in heaven or Father Abraham himself, who, now and then, visits a negro church and prays alongside his people.

We stand outside, gossiping and joking, as if green grass were underfoot instead of slush and lilacs bloomed in the dooryard instead of tiny flowers of frost. I'm made to feel one with the gay assembly. To hide runaways, to stand at a lectern at an abolitionists' meeting and speak of the negroes, to stop in the street a moment and chat with a freedman or a freedwoman—this is only to "speculate on the taste of a peach by looking at its skin," as Henry used to say. "You've got to take a bite out of it to *know*.

You've got to examine it *inside,* where the stone has bled into the flesh." I have not truly known negroes; I wonder if I ever will. They are familiar, yet alien— like this church, to be honest, which Father would call a "gospel mill."

Lucy and I go back inside, to find that boards have been laid across the chair backs and food is being set out on them. I eat the simple meal of bread fried in salt-pork drippings, pickled cabbage, and corn pudding. No one has touched the two dried fish, as if we are waiting for the Son of God to come and multiply them, as He did in a desert place to feed the five thousand.

"How you, Miss Lucy?" inquires a black woman wearing an old silk dress.

"Miss Selma, how should I be after Preacher gave old Satan the most awful castigation?"

"Preacher John do know how to pull the Devil's nose!"

"It's a wonder Lucifer ain't tired of tormenting colored folks!"

I marvel that Lucy, whom I've heard talk to the boys in the wards, is speaking like an unschooled negro washerwoman. I want to ask her which of the two voices is more natural to her, but I don't wish to offend. Suddenly I realize that I have more than one voice also, and could not say which of them is truly mine.

Miss Selma looks me in the eye and says, "Who might this be?"

"Miss Selma, I'd like you to meet my friend from the hospital, Miss Louisa Alcott."

"Miss Alcott." Miss Selma looks me in the eye again, and it is only now that I notice I tower above her. She is a woman who can look up at someone without giving an impression of submissiveness. I am made to feel as awkward as a giraffe among pygmies and as nervous as if they were armed with their little bows and poisoned arrows.

"What do you think of our church, Miss Alcott?"

"I didn't think much of it until I listened to Preacher John and heard you talking back and raising the roof with your singing and shouting. Now it doesn't seem so mean."

"The Spirit settled on you," says Miss Selma, folding her gnarled black hands over her stomach. My candor has disarmed her; she would have felt patronized had I spoken otherwise.

"Miss Louisa's an abolitionist," says Lucy, her eyes glinting with mischief. "She shared her crib with John Brown's daughters."

"My, my," responds Miss Selma, as if she'd been told that ice melts on a hot stove.

I feel my cheekbones rise, like those of an embarrassed child who has been chastened in adult company.

"Eat your pudding, Louisa," says Lucy, smiling.

Miss Selma calls across the room, "Preacher Holmes, come meet Miss Alcott."

Now it is for John Holmes to greet the interloper. No, Lu, that's unkind, since no one has made you feel anything but welcome. In fact, he says, "You are welcome, sister!" He holds out his hands. I put mine in his, as if entrusting myself to the Lord's care. Now it's my turn to look into another's eyes. Reflected in John Holmes's, which are purged of the rheum of shame, is the glory lent to lowly things by the Supreme Radiance. Not even Mr. Emerson ever made me feel this light, though Waldo's hands are not rough and calloused like this preacher's.

"What's in your heart, Miss Alcott?"

Without meaning to, I touch the place where my heart is.

"What do you feel, sister?" His eyes persist in sounding me.

I consider my answer carefully before deciding on what I hope will be the right words for the occasion. "I feel Him nigh." However, it's Henry whom I sense nearby—the Henry who led a runaway slave through the woods toward Canada. Waldo called Henry brave. (He said as much about Bronson. What a vexing man my father is—not all one thing or another!)

It is not in self-satisfaction that the preacher beams at me, but with joy that I have been warmed by the Holy Spirit. He leads me to the altar. For a moment, I think he means to induct me into the company of the righteous, and I wonder how to refuse his gift without offending him. I've struggled enough with my own uncertain spiritual condition to accept his Christ militant or a meek and gentle Lord on the strength of an hour's fellowship. But I'm mistaken; he means only to show me the altar cloth.

"These red stitches," he says. "Each stands for a fugitive slave who didn't get to cross the River Jordan." He means the Potomac. "God only knows how many died on the way here—shot by rebel soldiers, hanged or beaten to death by slave catchers, suffered unspeakable violence at the hands of some of our own soldiers, or just plain died of hunger, fever, or fear. There's no room to cast a stitch for everyone who didn't make it to the Promised Land. But God knows our hearts."

"God be praised!" cries Miss Selma.

"Amen!" replies Lucy, ringing her teacup with an old spoon.

I add nothing to the antiphony, but I hope that Holmes can see the contents of *my* heart with his sad beagle eyes. I never imagined that a black person's gaze could be so steady. It has always seemed to slide away from mine.

"Don't be afraid, Miss Alcott," says Holmes kindly.

I put out my hand and touch one of the red threads; I tremble, as though it were a wound impossible to heal. I quickly take my hand away.

He nods approvingly. "Deacon Smith," he calls to a middle-aged negro dressed in an old-fashioned frock coat.

"Reverend?" As he walks toward us, I note the patchwork on the tarnished garment. "Can I do somethin' for you?"

"Not for me, but can I ask you to drive these two ladies home?"

"They at Union Hospital?"

"They are. Would you be able to oblige them? It's a long way to go on a cold night. And bad men do not honor the Sabbath nor keep it holy."

"I am able, and glad."

Leaving is no small matter. Lucy and I become entangled in knots of well-wishers; hugs and kisses are exchanged, words of praise and comfort given. In the doorway, a black tide swells behind us, until we are disgorged into the front yard, where Deacon Smith and the buggy await. The horse regards us resentfully from underneath an ice-stiffened blanket. The rig belongs to the Willard Hotel. Mr. Smith works and sleeps in the livery stable.

"He didn't steal it, Louisa!" says Lucy, her eyes once again shiny with mischief. "The stable boss is a righteous man and lets the deacon take the buggy to church on Sunday evening."

Miss Selma calls to me, "Meet you at the River Jordan, Miss Alcott!"

The only Jordan that she will see is the creek up in

the Georgetown hills, where colored washerwomen have their shacks.

We sway through the evening gloom. Old black Charon sucks his briar. The smoke unfurls and mixes with the dusk. The giantess is still waiting in the snow. Big, brazen George Washington looks as if he wished to be elsewhere—at Fraunces Tavern in New York, perhaps, drinking maudlin farewell toasts with Continental army officers.

Sleep is tugging at my sleeve. Recite after me: A was an Archer, and shot at a frog, / B was a Blindman, and led by a dog, / C was a Cutpurse, and lived in disgrace, / D was a Drunkard, and had a red face.

Bless me, Father—

A buggy wheel jolts on a stone in the road, and I swim up from Lethe, to find my head on Lucy's shoulder. We're passing the President's House. The deacon takes off his hat in respect. I fancy I can see Mr. Lincoln at a lighted window, looking gravely at me. His sad eyes are sunk in their sockets. My eyes close slowly, and my chin rests in the knot of my scarf.

"Wake up, Louisa." Lucy is shaking me gently by the arm. "We're home."

Mother, is that Lizzie I see standing in the dooryard? The way she twirls her hair into a button at the back of her head, it must be she. Mother smiles and says, "Henry has brought her home from the Land of Egypt."

"Wake up now, miss!" says Lucy, pulling at my coat sleeve.

We thank Deacon Smith for having gone out of his way. He turns the horse around and heads back to the Willard brothers' stable. He leaves behind a fancy scroll of tobacco smoke. Louisa and I kiss each other's cheeks. I start for my attic bedroom, she for the scullery and the bed she shares with the colored cook.

Having put on my nightdress, I open my journal and turn to the fourteenth of March, 1858:

> My dear sister died at three this morning, after two years of patient pain. Last week she put her work away, saying the needle was "too heavy," and having given us her few possessions, made ready for the parting in her own simple, quiet way. For two days she suffered much, begging for ether, though its effect was gone. Tuesday she lay in Father's arms, and called us round her, smiling contentedly as she said, "All here!" I think she bid us good-by then, as she held our hands and kissed us tenderly. Saturday she slept, and at midnight became unconscious, quietly breathing her life away till three; then, with one last look of the beautiful eyes, she was gone.

Feeling the tooth of grief, I close the journal and lie down to sleep, which refuses me its balm. I remember Lizzie's funeral. In her coffin, she looked like a woman of sixty; she was not yet twenty-three. She was the prettiest of the Alcott girls. Waldo, Henry, Frank Sanborn, and John Pratt carried her from the hearse to the hole beside the ocher mound of earth.

Lizzie, I see you in your grave ravaged by "the Conqueror Worm!" Damn you, Poe, your morbidity, and you also, Edward Fenzil, for having brought him to mind after I'd shut him out, as one would an obnoxious guest! One can tell the story of a life right through to its end—to the deathbed and the howls of grief. To imagine the body after the last shovelful of earth has been thrown onto the coffin lid, however, is a desecration no better than robbing a grave!

Someday the worms will make a meal of me, I say in iambic pentameter. I can hear them laboring underground, eating the earth, to dig a grave for me, who need only be patient a little while. There are many ways to die, Lu, but you'll suffer only one of them and only once. That, my dear, is the gods' gift given to mortals.

WHILE PINNING UP MY HAIR, I recall a dream from the night just passed and confide it to my journal:

> January 11th—I went to the negro church nearby the creek. Much singing & jubilation, Amens!, Hallelujahs! &c. Abraham Lincoln arrived & stood beside Preacher Holmes. The president's

stovepipe hat rose into a smoky darkness—there appeared to be no ceiling, only a roiling of gray clouds, which I knew would smell of gunpowder. One by one, the people came forward & knelt before him. One by one, he touched their clouded eyes, & the scales fell from them. They shouted, "Hosanna!" & they cosseted the president, as if he were the Lamb. I noticed that his coat was torn & had made up my mind to mend it, when Lucy Higgs shook me awake.

When I see her in the ward, I take her aside to tell her of my dream. She is reserved, even cool toward me. I feel myself becoming angry and, biting my tongue, walk away. Later, I corner her on the stairs.

"Miss Higgs, have I offended you?" In truth, I'm the one who is offended.

Bowing her head, she studies the floor.

"Is something wrong with my shoes?" I am annoyed by her shiftiness, this person who, yesterday, looked me brazenly in the eye. She doesn't reply, so I slap her—not hard, but we are both taken by surprise. I address her like a stern schoolmistress to compose myself: "Lucy Higgs, whatever is the matter?"

"Now that you've seen me amongst my own people, I'm thinking you're embarrassed." She spoke in a curious tone, so that I can't decide whether I've been mocked by a pretense of hauteur or of humility—an ambivalence that makes me still angrier.

"What cause have I to be embarrassed?"

"I know how white people are when they see black folks carrying on."

"I wasn't aware of any 'carrying on.'" But having said that, I'm struck by the thought that I may have been embarrassed by their shouting and talking back, their moaning and praising, the squirming in their chairs when the Spirit was upon them, and the stale smell of unwashed bodies. In an atom of consciousness might I have been reminded of the vile odors of wounds, kitchens, washrooms, and stables with which I'm shut up all day long? Or is it something deeply buried and ancient that dismays me?

Niggers. The word appears—sudden and brutal—before me, as the "airy dagger" did to Macbeth. I recall Waldo saying, "What argument, what evidence can avail against the power of that one word *niggers*? The man of the world annihilates the whole combined force of all the antislavery societies of the world by pronouncing it."

ON ROCK CREEK, CHILDREN ARE SKATING in and out of the light cast by three bonfires. Like pilgrim planets orbiting the sun, they put on robes of molten gold, a radiance mortal children cannot bear too long before they must take them off again. Wearing his old shawl, has Mr. Lincoln turned from thoughts of cold immensity to investigate, with a telescope, a trio of new stars appearing low in the west? I close my eyes and see them blazing behind my lids. I see Jefferson Davis in Richmond, shouting huzzahs from the roof of his white house in the belief that Washington is burning, set alight by a secesh or a Locofoco Democrat.

Louisa, you should try to curb your imagination. Remember Mr. Field's admonishment: "Readers will not accept literary fantasy when the war news is incredible."

What seems now to have been incredible—a common occurrence at the time—was the sight of three literary lions skating on frozen Walden Pond. Mr. Emerson was serious, as if composing an essay in his head, Hawthorne skillful, and Henry about what you'd expect if the breath of life were blown into a scarecrow and a pair of skates strapped to its feet. I wonder at those days—at their ordinariness—whose significance I couldn't see. I see them now for what they are: pearls that I mistook for paste, heaped and forgotten in memory's casket. Henceforth, I will delight in each moment till time's conductor puts me off the train.

Except for the hissing and scratching of their skate blades on Rock Creek ice, the children are quiet. Do they fear deserters, who move about at night? Or can it be they've stolen from their houses, where their fearful parents keep them shut up till morning, to pass a silent night among their friends? (How we love to be with our own kind!) I've seen few children since my arrival in Georgetown. Until this moment, I wasn't really aware of their absence. My attention has been fixed on the soldiers in the wards and in the streets and on the grave men who decide their fates or profit by them.

We call the sick and wounded men "our boys"; I've heard one nurse speak of them as "her babies." I don't expect to be a mother, save for the children I imagine into being and put on paper, but the impulse to hold a helpless being to my breast, stroke his fever-dampened hair, and dry his tears is strong in me. Not that the men do much crying. Only when the pain is unbearable will they cry out for the ether sponge, laudanum, or whiskey if nothing stronger can be had. John Sulie never shed a tear, although he knew that he had climbed into his deathbed.

I picture the child skaters turning from the light and, as though hearing a sound inaudible to grown-ups, chasing it into the darkness. They zigzag up the creek until they disappear, never to return, like the children of Hamelin in thrall to the Pied Piper, who took them in revenge for their parents' broken pledge. Remember, Lu, the stanza in Robert Browning's poem?

> . . . the Piper advanced and the children
>   followed,

And when all were in to the very last,
The door in the mountain-side shut fast.

Oh, how I'd love to see an uprising in the "children's" ward! "Rise, take up thy bed, and walk!" I see the boys throw off the shroudlike sheets, kick over the chamber pots, pick up their crutches, and walk—or hop—out of the House of Pain. They won't stop until they have reached the place where "the wolf also shall dwell with the lamb, and the leopard shall lie down with the kid; and the calf and the young lion and the fatling together; and a little child shall lead them."

With lighted lamp, I pass among the sleepers and know myself to be a far cry from Florence Nightingale, adored by sick and wounded men in Constantinople as "the Lady with the Lamp." The boys call me "the Lady with the Bottle" because of the lavender water I carry through the wards to mitigate a stink that "all the perfumes of Arabia would not sweeten." Nor can all the camphor bags in Christendom, hung around the necks of young men by their wives and mothers, ward off the fevers and distempers of the blood that lay waste to more soldiers than does the sum of rebel army ordnance.

After I've visited my portion of the eighty beds at Union Hospital and tended the sick with basin and sponge, I say to myself, Lu, you've done the human wash and laid it out to dry. The patriots are asleep—not a one is a scoundrel, Dr. Johnson. I lay nosegays of heliotrope on their pillows. If their dreams cannot be sweet, may they be fragrant. It is night when I feel the least martial. I wish for home—even such homes as the Alcott women have called their own.

How quietly the soldiers sleep tonight! I strain to hear a moan, a whimper, or a fragment of gibberish uttered in a dream, but only a light snoring—the universal anthem of exhausted men—and the sound of water dripping from a tap impair an almost perfect silence.

Would the Germans Marx and Engels manage things better, in a world where every man is at his neighbor's throat? The Communist Manifesto repudiates slavery. And yet I was a child slave in Father's arcadia, Fruitlands, which nearly broke the Alcotts into pieces. Hawthorne, who paid for the privilege of spreading manure from dawn till dusk, came to despise George Ripley's communal dream of Brook Farm. Utopias thrive on paper, even as they degenerate into tyranny or simply wither in the actual world of men and women. Perhaps words are ineffectual and those smitten by them impractical idealists or fools.

Are you, in your idealism, a fool, Mr. Emerson?

Louisa, you're tired. To bed with you and save a sprig of heliotrope to lay beside your head.

THIS MORNING, I HAVE COME with Fanny, Anna Miller, and Ida Crane to the cemetery to pay our last respects to Mr. Olson, whose given name is—or was—Albert. One is never sure of the tense in cases of the recently departed, whom the newspapers call "the late," as if referring to someone habitually unpunctual. Albert lived with his invalid mother somewhere on Congress Street, near the Chesapeake and Ohio Canal. What the poor man may have hoped to find in his youthful days, who can tell? All that can be said is that he found, in his diurnal round, sickness, debility, and death. I saw him only a few times and never once did I speak to him. From all appearances, he was shy around women and not much livelier around men. I scarcely noticed him until the day he was boiled alive. Forgive me, Albert. Perhaps I thought time would bring us together, as it has—here and now—at your grave. (More likely, I was consumed by my own thoughts and projects.)

The here and now is a difficult place to occupy. My mind slips away from the sight of Earth's raw and gaping wound in Oak Hill Cemetery to that at Sleepy Hollow, where my sister was laid to rest. Tell it true, Louisa! Where my sister (she was dear to me, and sweet) was put into the dirt, which was shoveled rudely over her. Mourners ought never stand next to a loved one's grave while the diggers fill the hole they made. There is no gentle way to do their awful business or to muffle the thuds resounding on a coffin lid. The grave is no "wondrous portal opened wide" to receive the lost children of Hamelin, and no beguiling melody is heard inside the cavern to cheer us with thoughts of immortality.

Yet when Mother and I wept over Lizzie at the instant she went silent and felt the chill of fading life, we saw a light mist rising from the dear body—a husk left by the awful winnowing of Death. Softly, she withdrew beyond Mother's homeopathic science and the virtue of her much-thumbed variorum *The Organon of the Healing Art*. Turning to Dr. Geist for confirmation of our senses, he said with an awful simplicity, "It is her life departing visibly."

Father was elsewhere, overseeing the renovations to Orchard House, which he purchased with a five-hundred-dollar loan from Mr. Emerson. (Had there been no Emerson, America would have lacked a moral philosopher, and the Alcotts an almoner and most loyal friend.)

In Oak Hill Cemetery, I lift up my eyes unto the man of God, whose own are glazed as he conducts Mr. Olson to his afterlife. I've seen the same blissful face on surgeons as they ponder a complicated amputation. Over the minister's bald head, which is perspiring in spite of the cold, I see the vulcanized time ball slowly descending on its staff atop the observatory dome.

IN THE HOSPITAL REFECTORY, I sit down to the usual breakfast of fried beef, salt butter, husky bread, and washy coffee, along with eight other women, who natter about nothing, and a dozen men absorbed in their own affairs. I don't care to linger, because one or another of them is bound to remark, "Watch out; that child's among us, taking notes." If they only knew how poorly they fare in my journal!

Fanny Warren rushes into the dining room. "Louisa! Julius is in that awful place again!"

"Not in the cellar hole?"

"What should we do?" Her appeal, like her gaze, is directed at all of us, but none of the masticators, swallowers, or gossipers takes any notice.

"We must tell Matron Ropes!" I am emphatic, hoping to shame the others, whose eyes are now fixed on their plates. "Let's go, Fanny," I say, glaring at them.

The hospital steward punishes any sick or wounded soldier he considers troublesome by locking him in the unlighted cellar. He also steals clothes, soap, and food intended for the patients. He means to profit by the war and once offered Mrs. Ropes a share in his pilferage for her connivance. She complained to the hospital's chief surgeon, Dr. Clark, who cares too much for the bottle to intervene, and wrote to Surgeon General Hammond, who replied that she must prove her accusations.

"I won't put up with it!" exclaims the matron,

who tears off her eyeglasses and puts down the morning paper. "I have no office to lose or gain. I am free to do right, and if any patient in this house is put into that black hole, I will go to Washington and stay until I gain the 'open sesame' to that door. I'll call at the office of Secretary of War Stanton, if need be!"

We hurry down the cellar steps and let the poor man out of the vermin-infested hole. He shakes with fever and mutters in Low German his thanks to God for not having abandoned him. I'd like to tell him that he owes his gratitude not to God, whose ears are stuffed with ticking, but to Mrs. Ropes, but I've no wish to offend her by blaspheming. The woman is a saint. As a rule, I disapprove of saints and find their company dull, but the matron's compassion is of the exceptional kind rarely found in ordinary mortals. I'd ask the Almighty to bless her, but since He did not see fit to save my sister Lizzie, regardless of my prayers and entreaties, I doubt He would oblige me in this.

When the soldier steps into the light coming in at the head of the stairs, we notice a gash on his cheek. Fearing a reprisal, he won't say what caused the wound, but we press him until he admits that the steward hit him with a chisel.

"Julius will be better off at Armory Square Hospital. Let me write a note of explanation for Superintendent Dix, and then you two can escort him there."

"My thanks, Matron," says the wounded man,

who begins to sob. What would the stoic Marcus Aurelius have made of these tears? I don't give a damn for the manly tribe, whose skins are thick and hearts are hard! Give me the weepy Greek Achilles, who cried for his dead friend. Tears are the solvent in which the stony hearts of men dissolve. Lu, that's wishful thinking, as well you know!

Dorothea Dix receives us cordially. She is a kind old soul, but very queer and arbitrary. I see nothing dragonish about her, and we soon find a bed for Julius. A surgeon examines him, cleans and bandages his wounded cheek, and, after feeling his forehead, prescribes calomel and rest. Fanny locates a Lutheran chaplain, and having delivered our abused patient's body and soul to a cleaner, more salubrious place in which to convalesce, we put on our cloaks and wish Miss Dix a good day.

As we are leaving the ward, I happen to see Walt Whitman carrying a slop jar. I didn't notice before how broad his shoulders are and how attractively he carries himself, although he does affect a devil-may-care attitude, which I find laughable.

"Fanny, so long as we're this side of Rock Creek, what do you say to a small adventure?"

"Won't we be missed?" she asks with an apprehension that makes me, who feels none, superior to her.

"We'll blame it on *force majeure*." She cocks her

head like a common wren addressed by a wise old owl. "Circumstances beyond our control."

She agrees, and we plunge into the cold midday air, arm in arm and our wind-chafed faces wreathed in smiles.

ON MISSOURI AVENUE, ACROSS THE CANAL from the gasworks, Fanny and I step into a lunchroom noisy with men whose clothes are in need of airing. They have the look of underlings in the hierarchy of privilege, which towers above them like Mount Everest. I take note of one man in particular, who appears neither hangdog nor bumptious, sitting apart from the rest and quietly eating sausage and peas.

Fanny and I order potato soup, bread, and, since we are teetotalers, coffee. We collect our thoughts like scattered parcels as men, horses, and conveyances pass by in the street. Before their fall, the imperial cities of the ancient world would have bustled just so with soldiers, statesmen, charlatans, and opportunists. In a thousand years will Washington City be known by its cracked walls and broken paving stones? Will archaeologists speculate on the significance of a replica of a man in a tricornered hat astride a horse—the name WASHINGTON worn by winds blowing for a millennium? Perhaps it will take us only a century to reach the Everest of our greatness before we tumble down into the dust. The insect kingdoms erect their hills and hives and believe in their everlasting glory, unaware of how briefly they reign and little they accomplish. At this moment in Richmond is a woman staring out the window at a street crowded with men in gray uniforms and frock coats, her head filled with thoughts that may be vainglorious, mean-spirited, ambitious, or funereal? Would I see myself in her, and she in me?

"Louisa, your soup is getting cold," says Fanny, who has started on hers. "'Eat and get the benefit of it hot' is what my mother always says."

I dawdle over the bowl with my spoon. "Your mother sounds like my father, full of sound advice as welcome as Polonius's was to Laertes." I regret the bitterness of my voice not because it dishonors my father, who is pompous, but because it does Fanny's mother, who may be truly wise. Wisdom is not exclusive to Concord, nor is every sage a man.

She takes no notice of my harsh tone. She is talking about her childhood in Lowell, where her father worked in a cotton mill till he died of pleurisy. Her mother took over his loom and will no doubt cough herself to death in a year or two or ten.

I remember having visited the town with Father. He thought he might open a school for the mill hands' children, the few who didn't need to work. We made the twenty-mile trip on the Boston and Low-ell Railroad. While Father met with the clergy and some of the families, I ran along the bluffs above the

Merrimack, on which Henry and his brother, John, had rowed and sailed to the White Mountains. I think I must have been a deer or a horse in some former state, because it is such a joy for me to run. Not long after my arrival in Washington, I resumed my early-morning pastime. After being questioned by a policeman who thought me suspicious, I gave it up. I swear, there's no better tonic for stifled lungs than to go full chisel when the sun begins to rise!

"Aren't you hungry, Louisa?"

"No."

"You look peaked." She lays a hand on my forehead. "You don't feel warm."

"I'm not sick, Fanny, just low in spirit."

"I expect it's the war," she says, her expression composed of sagacity and solicitude.

"I expect you're right." She's too good-hearted and well-meaning for me to scorn her diagnosis. It would take more penetrating eyes than her cornflower blue ones to see to the bottom of my malaise, which is a modern word for the soul's unease. You'd need a Transcendentalist or a mesmerist, I tell myself, amused—or a nihilist like Edward Fenzil or Edgar Poe. (Dr. Mütter would not find it any more than he could a pigeon's compass with his scalpel and probe.) I eat some bread to please Fanny while I try to unthread the several voices from the tangle of contrary opinions in the room.

"Burnside ought to be taken out and shot after the mess at Fredericksburg!"

"They should hang him by his fool side-whiskers."

"We'd have won the damn war already if it weren't for McClellan!"

"Little Mac did what he had to," opines a large man as he wipes a spill of gravy from his lapel.

"Skedaddle, retreat, and run like hell!"

"It was Old Fuss and Feathers left the ball."

"You mean Old Fat and Feeble. Pierce ought to have given him Mexico to play with instead of the Army of the Potomac."

"Tell you what," says a thin-faced man with too many teeth. "We ought to take up a collection and send Ape Lincoln to Africa; let him be king of the monkeys and the niggers."

"You sound secesh!" barks a lieutenant of the First Regiment, District of Columbia, laying a hand on his sword hilt.

"He sounds like a goddamn traitor!" exclaims a clerking type in a threadbare suit.

"I'm just saying what a whole lot of people think."

The soldier and the clerk have gotten to their feet. The landlord gathers up the glasses, as a hen would her chicks. "Take it outside!" he growls.

I've forgotten about the man eating sausage and peas until he, too, has gotten to his feet. Not pausing to remove the napkin tucked into his collar, he strides across the floor and pokes a Derringer into the belly

of the provocateur. Only when I hear a caisson rat-
tling down Missouri Avenue do I realize how hushed
the room is as we await the outcome of hostilities on a
miniature battlefield demarcated by a grimy window,
the cashier's counter, and a row of coats resembling
men hanged en masse from pegs. Fanny giggles nervously, and a man wearing a purple waistcoat coughs.

The toothy troublemaker swats stupidly at the
pistol pointed at his belly. On the wall behind his
head, a flyspecked chromo memorializes the burning
of the President's House by the British.

"Mister, I'd be careful if I was you," warns the
vigilante as he yanks the napkin from his shirt collar and wipes his upper lip. His fastidiousness strikes
me as remarkable. Lu, you must remember it; vivid
details make a piece seem real. "One of you boys get
a copper. Tell him William P. Wood, superintendent
of the Old Capital Prison, has caught a traitor."

"Mr. Wood," I call in a steady voice that belies
the roaring in my ears.

"Ma'am?"

"Is it all right if my friend and I leave?"

"By all means do."

Fanny and I hurry into our capes and are out the
door and halfway to Pennsylvania Avenue before we
realize we didn't pay for our meals.

"I promised you an adventure, and we had one," I
say to Fanny, whose color has returned to her cheeks.

"One I could live without. I'm not brave like you."

"Timid girls don't pack a trunk and travel by steamer, train, and car to sponge some poor boy's stumps!"

"Sometimes you're so fierce, Louisa, you frighten me!"

"When you've lived as many places as you have years and have been put to work as a seamstress, teacher, farmer, and skivvy, you learn to take a harsh view of life." Maybe not so harsh as clearheaded. Of the people I've known, Henry Thoreau saw things clearest. For all his profundity, Mr. Emerson's view is too rosy, Hawthorne's too melancholy, and my father's too idealistic. Edward Fenzil, whom I didn't have time to know, has the same morbid cast as did his master Poe. I would have found his friendship difficult, perhaps, in time, even repugnant. Only Henry seemed to draw breath in an atmosphere like sweet water. To be with him was to share, however briefly and imperfectly, in the limpidity of being that Buddhists and shamans are said to possess. Of course, I was only a girl at the time and easily swayed.

"Louisa, is your heart set on visiting Mr. Brady's? I'm feeling done in."

"I want a copy of Gardner's photograph of us in the ward."

"Whatever for, Louisa? It's sure to be ghastly!"

To include in my book about Hurly-burly House. Let Boston and Concord see the gender of its author! "Come on, Fanny! A walk in the cold air will perk you up."

FANNY AND I STOP FOR A TROOP of cavalry passing Brown's Hotel. The men and the horses in their iron shoes give up the ghost through their mouths and noses in the icy wind blowing from the Potomac. (I don't believe in portents, except for those in Shakespeare's plays.) We locate the National Photographic Art Gallery on the avenue at number 625, hurry into the foyer, stamp our boots to rid them of snow, and climb the unswept staircase to Mathew Brady's studio. A man wearing sleeve protectors answers my knock, and, without waiting to be invited inside, I drag Fanny to the stove.

"Good afternoon, ladies." The man is—Oh, what's the smug word Whitman favors? *Imperturbable*. Quite right, Louisa!

"Good afternoon, Mr. Brady."

"What can I do for you besides sharing my stove?"

"You must think us a pair of Tartars or Christian Temperance zealots come to smash up the furniture, but my friend and I just had supper in a madhouse."

"All of Washington is one." He smiles, and I feel embarrassed.

"I wish to purchase one of the images that Mr. Gardner made on Tuesday at Union Hospital."

"Ah! Then you two must be nurses."

"As you can see by the way we're dressed," I say a trifle too flippantly. I introduce us. "My friend Miss Warren; I am Miss Alcott, lately of Concord."

"You'll be more comfortable if you take off your capes and hats. Once it gets going, the stove is hot as Nebuchadnezzar's furnace."

At the mention of the Babylonian king who commanded that Hebrew captives Shadrach, Meshach, and Abednego be cast into a furnace for refusing to bow to his graven image, my mind falls back, with the swiftness of recollection, to another winter—that of 1851, when the fate of a runaway black from Norfolk, Virginia, was the talk of Boston. If I lend an ear to the muffled commotion of the past, I hear, again, words from a song that was often heard on street corners and in barrooms when the doors swung open.

"Shadrach and Liberty,
Webster and Slavery!"

Chanting them, we watched as a band of free black men and abolitionists emancipated Shadrach Minkins from the Boston courthouse and helped him on his way to Canada. Shame on Daniel Webster for using his silver tongue to praise the Fugitive Slave Act! May he be damned to speak eternally to an empty hall! By that ignominious law, runaway slaves would be returned to their "owners," even those who had taken up new lives as freedmen in the North. And if it please you, God, condemn Chief Justice Taney to an afterlife of crawling on his belly in a briar patch in Hell for having ordered Dred Scott returned to bondage and—for the advancement of white supremacy—defining negroes "as beings of an inferior order, altogether unfit to associate with the white race"!

Brady hangs our things on a coat tree, sets two cane chairs by the glowering stove, and bids us sit. We do and smooth our skirts.

"Would you like some tea?" He seems as determined to be polite as I have been to be rude. I wonder why I should feel the need to make myself disagreeable. Not even Hawthorne could see into the darkness of a heart whose chambers are shut. (Few could see into his—that taciturn man so difficult to like.)

"No, thank you. Perhaps Miss Warren would." I suspect she'd like something to occupy her hands, which are like two small birds nervously hopping in her lap.

"Yes, please."

Brady takes a cast-iron pan from the stove and sprinkles tea leaves on the boiling water. "You're sure you won't have any, Miss Alcott? You'll see your future at the bottom of the cup."

My future, I hope, will be to get out from under all that crushes me.

"Thank you, no." I find myself wishing for something hot to drink but remain steadfast to my first impulse. I don't want him to mistake me for a woman who doesn't know her own mind.

He sets a taboret beside Fanny and gets a mismatched cup and saucer from a shelf. His attentiveness plainly embarrasses her.

"Strong or weak, Miss Warren?"

"Middling."

Henceforth, you shall be known as "Miss Middling." Don't be unkind, Louisa! You can't expect a woman from Lowell to be as decisive as one from Concord, where the mind of Waldo Emerson revolves like a compass needle hunting for the Absolute.

"Middling it is." He takes the pan from the stove and pours the steaming tea through a strainer into Fanny's cup.

For just a moment, her hand shakes, and I hold my breath, fearing that she will spill it on her lap. Mr. Olson's scalding was enough.

The mismatched crockery speaks of a laudable absence of ostentation in the man, rather than of an impoverished household like the Alcotts'. (In his tiny cabin, Henry had only two cups, to keep his "dinner parties" small.)

Brady's gallery is clean and tidy, the floor swept, and the furniture efficiently arranged. The photographs on the walls are aligned with mathematical nicety. He catches me looking at them.

"You won't find it there, Miss Alcott." He takes an exposed negative from a drawer and puts it in my lap. "I haven't had time to make a print."

I hold the glass plate to the light shed by an oil

lamp and squint. To look at it gives me an unpleasant sensation having nothing to do with the grim scene, which, frankly, I can't make out.

"Like seeing your own ghost," he says. He takes the sooty-looking negative from me and examines it through a loupe. "Mr. Gardner knows his business." He offers the glass plate and the loupe to Fanny, who declines, as if afraid of what she may see. He studies the negative again. "I assure you, Miss Alcott, that he has done you and your friend justice. I'll send two prints to the hospital as soon as I can get to them."

I'm aware that he has been glancing sidelong at Fanny with a frankness that verges on impertinence. Before I can reprove him, he asks her if she wouldn't mind sitting for a portrait.

Blushing, she turns to me for an opinion, which I withhold. I confess to feeling slighted, although I know she is handsomer than I am. No, Lu, you are *handsome*; Fanny is pretty.

"I suppose it would be all right," she says, left to "fix her own flint," as the boys say.

"Good!" He puts a chair underneath a skylight. "Sit here, Miss Warren."

I go and take a closer look at the photographs on the wall, while Brady directs Fanny to strike a pose, alter it, arrange the folds of her dress, smooth her hair, lift her chin, turn it slightly to the left, then to the right. "Fix your bosom, Miss Warren. It's all bunched up." I picture the flush creeping up Fanny's neck from beneath her starched collar.

An image catches my eye—a portrait of Walt Whitman gazing insolently toward his posterity. His glance insists that posterity should be admiring and grateful. As I look into his eyes, so candid and assured, I notice something beyond the folderol. I have been revising my opinion of Whitman—though not of his poetry—ever since Matron Ropes grudged him her approval because of his visits to the wards, good cheer, words of comfort, and the small gifts he freely distributes to the sick and wounded, both Northerners and Southerners. (There is one long-legged Johnny Reb in whose scornful eyes I'd like to rub soap. But I recognize in him the United States of pain and suffering.)

"That's Walt Whitman," says Brady, who has left Fanny sitting stiffly, her head gripped by an iron clamp. "A poet. I think a great one. Do you know him?"

"No."

"I'm surprised you don't recognize the face; he's a frequent visitor to the hospitals."

"They're thousands of doctors, nurses, attendants, porters, missionaries, and visitors in Washington."

"You couldn't miss this fellow; he's six feet tall."

Why not admit that you know him, Louisa, at least by sight and reputation?

"His verses are not for a young woman—but I

guess you've seen enough by now not to be shocked by mere words."

What is it the soldiers say of those who've seen the ghastly things men do to one another?

"I've seen the elephant, Mr. Brady."

He laughs delightedly.

Wanting to be rid of him, I point to Fanny. "Poor Miss Warren looks uncomfortable."

"In a minute, Miss Warren." I sense the pressure of his gaze. "You have a steely quality, Miss Alcott, not unlike the indomitable Clara Barton." He nods his head toward a photograph of the woman who trailed her skirts through mud and gore at First Bull Run and Antietam. "I didn't see your backbone at first, only your insolence. Would you allow me to photograph you after your friend?"

"I think not, Mr. Brady," I reply with a firmness I don't wholly feel.

"May I know the reason?"

Since I have no good reason to give, I make one up. "I'm too shy."

"You aren't, you know," he says, eyeing me shrewdly.

Returning to Fanny, he summarily uncaps the camera lens, counts, and then covers it. He appears to have lost interest in her as a subject, but he promises to send her a pack of *cartes-de-visite* for her pains.

"And Miss Alcott, you shall have your photograph, as well."

I shrug, and in the dismissive gesture, I feel the pleasure that men must take in it.

I MOUSE ABOUT THE WARDS, feeling small. I tend to a Union soldier with a bullet in his lung and a Confederate sharpshooter who might have put it there. To each, I say a kind word. Even the long-legged Johnny Reb whose haughty disdain usually infuriates me receives a smile and a bag of sweets from the Lady with the Bottle. I am mellowing and hope to be a ripe and sweet old pippin before this war is finished.

Before going to bed, I write to Mr. Emerson:

> Union Hospital
> Georgetown
> January 18, 1863

Dear Mr. Emerson,

Life here at the hospital does not so much go on, as it lurches like a locomotive seeking purchase on a slippery track. In other words, we live by fits & starts—just the thing for a diarist, but I find that my journal entries since leaving Boston are sparse. The nurse's calling is peremptory—I can advance this as a reason for my feeling somewhat "off" words, which a man spoke of as "mere." Well, perhaps he is unacquainted with yours, friend, or Henry's. I miss him sorely, as I know you & Lidian do. He was Master of our Revels, in my Concord Days.

You, Waldo, were Master of my Reveries.

The war discourages pretentiousness, although I've met a few shallow, silly fellows & have heard of a great many others. I wish you could have spoken to a young blacksmith from Virginia, who died nobly during my first week here. His name was John Sulie. I write it down, for if anyone deserves remembrance, it is he.

John, you will have two resting places: in the burial ground where your forebears lie and in my breast. No, Louisa, no! You must rid your thoughts—and prose—of treacle!

I've seen many great people in Boston and in Washington & found them to be no bigger than a frog in a pond filled with toads—& not half so good as some humble soul who makes no noise.

Did you know Walt Whitman is here? I've seen him several times at Hurly-burly House, as I call Union Hospital, & at Armory Square, where he spends many of his days. He does much good, & though he tends to prink & strut, his heart is large. I've made up my mind to introduce myself. I'll give him your regards, if you've forgiven him. Tell me if you have.

Louisa

Faces crowd my memory. I pick Lizzie's from the jostling figures and try to dwell on it, but it has already begun to fade, like a glass-plate negative left out in the sun. In time, the memory of our days together will transpire like attar pressed from petals in the Valley of the Rose. It will perfume the pages of the book I've yet to discover in myself. No, Miss Alcott! If you're to be faithful to the age, your pages must not smell of roses, but of human blood and excrement! Woe to Mr. Fields and his genteel readers! I will give you the book you want, James T. Fields! I'll electrify your hair and singe your pharisaical beard!

I snuff out the candles and get into the narrow bed and wait for sleep to overtake me.

Jolted from sleep by the clatter of a dropped basin, I light the candle and, waving it around the attic room, as if to scare the roaches back into the cracks in the wall, I see Miss Crawford lying on the floor.

"Mattie, what's wrong?" I ask as my heart beats loudly in its cage. Her hair is damp, her head hot to the touch; blood is running from her nose. I get her into bed and staunch the flow with cotton lint. I throw my robe over my nightdress and hurry downstairs, where I find one of the doctors at a desk, his head resting on his arms. I shake him till he wakes.

He rubs his tired eyes with the heels of his hands. "What is it, Miss Alcott?" Knowing his weariness, I overlook his peevish tone.

"Mattie Crawford. I think she has typhoid."

He gets his bag and follows me to the attic. Feverish, Mattie is moaning. I put my ear to her lips, but she is speaking a solfeggio of mad syllables, as if Pentecostal fire were falling on her. Pushing me aside, Dr. Reston touches her forehead, takes the pulse at her wrist, and feels her abdomen, which, he says, is distended. He presses it again, and she yelps in pain.

"Throw some light here!" he orders as he unbuttons her nightdress. "See that?" By the wavering candlelight, I see dark spots, which, by day, would be the color of a crimson rose—the visiting card left by typhoid fever. From the Valley of the Rose!

"They don't usually show themselves till the second week. Has she been sick?"

"She's been complaining of a headache and stomach pain. She's seemed worn-out lately, but we all have been since Fredericksburg."

"We'll quarantine her here, where you can look after her."

"Yes, Doctor." My gaze shifts from his and settles on the place where I had tried to dig out the deathwatch beetle with a pen, of which Henry had once written:

> Nor can all the vanities that vex the world
> alter one whit the measure that night has

chosen. Every pulse-beat is in the exact
time with the cricket's chant and the
tickings of the death-watch in the wall.

"Sponge her down and keep her covered; you
know what to do—and for God's sake, shut the
window!"

Contrite for having insisted that it remain open,
to rid the room of the vile odors wafting from the
washrooms, I gently close it.

"Do what you can for her, Miss Alcott," he says
in a kindlier tone.

I draw a chair to her bed, wet her lips, and wait.

In the morning, a surgeon looks in on her. The
fever hasn't broken, although her brow is not so hot as
the griddle it felt like during the night. She still wears
the rose-colored spots on her chest.

"Were you able to get any sleep, Nurse Alcott?"

"A little. She was mumbling in hers."

"That's the fever talking. We need to keep her
well watered."

Mattie's eyes are shut. She is picking at the bedclothes, as if to rid them of nits. I give her a moistened
cloth to suck, which she takes like an eager infant
blindly nursing at its mother's breast, and like one,
she makes small sounds of contentment. Her eyelids
twitch in the grip of "nervous fever."

"Get some fresh air into your lungs. I'll send
another nurse to sit with her."

I put on a doubtful face to hide my wish to be

away from the sickroom and out of doors. Hungrily, I look at the new snow piled on the window ledge. "If you think it'll be all right . . ."

"Get some air," he repeats. "You look played out."

"The cold air will perk me up!" I chirp. I need more than perking to restore the abruptly altered heart skipping beats inside my tightened chest.

"Eat something. You'll come down with a fever yourself if you let your constitution weaken."

I go downstairs to the refectory and eat the unsavory food and swallow the thin coffee.

"I didn't see Mattie last night or this morning," says Anna Miller, who arrived in town not long after I did. She's a lively girl, whom the boys in the wards adore for her pert tongue and pleasing shape. The older nurses, the pious, dowdy ones, dismiss her as a "saucebox," who ought to have stayed home in Scranton, sewed havelocks, and prayed.

"I'm afraid she's got typhoid," I say, embarrassed by my eagerness to leave her bedside.

"The poor soul!" says Anna, whose sympathy is real.

"I've an errand to run for the matron," I say, lying. I hunger to get away from Hurly-burly House, if only for a few hours—a hunger no amount of beefsteak and oysters can appease.

Anna squeezes my wrist, as though to wring out the truth, but it's solicitude she intends to convey by the gesture.

I excuse myself and leave by the kitchen door, intending to turn my back awhile on the city and tramp westward to the banks of the Potomac, beyond which the gin of war is separating men's souls from their harrowed bodies. Were I to trade my pen for a soothsayer's crystal, I'd see the world in ruins—a paradise for archaeologists, if *Homo sapiens* survives, or an annex of Hell, if it doesn't. More likely, Washington will serve as our fallen empire's necropolis. The buildings already resemble those of antiquity—so they seem to me, who once turned the pages of Vitruvius's *De architectura* in the Boston Athenaeum. How marvelous are the days of peace, which is, sadly, no longer with us!

Bundled against the wind, I walk down Jefferson Street to the dirt path beside the "Grand Old Ditch." I make for the Aqueduct Bridge—said to be a marvel—which joins the Chesapeake and Ohio Canal at Georgetown and the Alexandria Canal. Ahead, I see eight massive piers rise out of the bed of the river, which the bridge's granite icebreakers part. As I draw near, the graceful arches and delicate trusses that uphold the aerial waterway come into view. North of the bridge, on the Union side of the Potomac, earthen fortifications stand ready to repel a rebel attack on Washington from the west. On the river's far shore, Virginia shelters Lee's formidable army. At Richmond, a hundred miles from where I stand, Jefferson Davis makes his wishes known to the eleven

Confederate States of America by post, telegraph, dispatch riders, and secret agents of both sexes.

I am beside the great bridge; its cold shadow covers me. I hear voices as Henry heard on Mount Ktaadn—rumors of "Chaos and ancient Night." I shiver for a complicated knot of causes, impossible to untangle. In my thoughts, I compose a letter to Henry, who is beyond the reach of postmen.

January 19, 1863

Dear Friend,

I'm standing on a verge seemingly as definitive as the one you crossed in May. Behind me is the imperial city; in front of me, across the river, which once belonged to the aborigines, is another kind of empire, one smelling of the soil and its fruits, as well as fear and human toil.

I suddenly see our years in Walden Woods, on the pond, and at Mr. Emerson's "salon" as a tableau prettily arranged—a robin's egg the jay has overlooked. But it has found the egg and is cracking it with a rapacity you would hardly recognize in your former countrymen.

Do you play the flute for the cherubim? Do you dance in your big boots before the throne of God—or that of Jove, Jupiter, Osiris, Indra, or the Crow Mother of the Hopi? It matters not at all so long as your heart beats the measure and the tune is sweet.

Except for an open channel midway between the banks, the river is frozen. I imagine that a Fitchburg Railroad train could run across the Concord River in January and never get its wheels wet. Winter here is undeserving of the name to one who is New England–bred, yet I'm cold in the marrow of my bones.

I'll write you again and soon, Henry dear, though the mail service between my country and yours is unreliable, which is the reason I've not heard from you since you went "berrying" in the spring.

Lu

I leave the Aqueduct Bridge, a Xanadu built not by Kublai Khan but by William Turnbull and the Army Corps of Engineers, and walk south toward Mason's Island and the colored troops. The shore resembles an arctic waste. The salt grass is tarnished gold; the trees are spangled. Except for a solitary cardinal whose whipstitched flight appears like a scarlet thread on a white sheet (or the altar cloth in the negro church behind the railroad depot), there is nothing quick to see. You've come to the end of the world, Lu. Who knew it lay so near?

At the island's northern end, on a gravel bar where scrub oak and locust lean over the roiling water, I see a ragged heap. Whether it is flotsam, an ice floe cut by the granite footings of the bridge up above, or a corpse, I'm too far away to tell.

I have never looked through a camera lens. Does it make people look small or big? I've heard that it turns them upside down. If I were to photograph the islet and the scraggly tree whose bare branches dip toward the river like divining rods, what would I see captured in its net of branches? Could it be a man? What sort of man? What is a man in a photograph, which is a kind of memory? What is a man who exists only in memory, like my Henry and my brave and noble John?

Louisa, mind your mind; it's running away with you again! It's not a corpse you see in the river, but a mound of dirty snow.

It is a man.

You see nothing, Lu, because there's nothing to see in the universal night, which is falling in spite of the weak sun overhead. If you were standing not in snow but in some summer field, you would see a heap of cut grass left by the mower—Whitman's "hopeful green stuff," which hides wounds made by cannon shot and grave diggers' spades.

It is some dead thing.

I tell you, Louisa, it is only the light on the river, playing tricks on your eyes—the somber light falling on dirty snow transmogrified by your frayed nerves into something morbid. In your mind's eye, the scenes of slaughter displayed on Mathew Brady's wall persist.

"Mere words," Mr. Brady? When flesh disintegrates, words are all that's left to us, and of us all.

Dispirited, I trudge back to Union Hospital.

MATTIE'S BED IS STRIPPED OF SHEETS, the window open to air out the room. Only the muffled drumbeat of a heart in mourning for itself disturbs the silence as I strain to hear a human sound. I go downstairs and hunt among the wards for Dr. Reston, who is nowhere to be found. I corner the matron in her dismal office.

"Where is Nurse Crawford?" I hear the anger in my voice.

"I sent her to Armory Square Hospital, where she can be better seen to. Sit down, Miss Alcott; you look all in."

I sit and bite my lip, as if waiting for a judgment to be passed.

"She took a turn for the worse. She has a better chance of recovering at Armory Square, where it's cleaner and airier." Reading my thoughts, she takes my wrist. "She's not dead, Louisa. She's in quarantine."

I picture Walt Whitman standing above Mattie, his great shaggy head tilted to one side, his sympathies comprehensive and genuine.

"Do you feel up to accompanying Dr. McClintock to Mason's Island? A negro soldier there is too gravely wounded to bring in by ambulance. I wouldn't ask if I had another nurse to send."

I say to myself, No, Matron, I'm not up to it at all. I feel the oddest sensation.

Aloud, I reply, "Yes, Matron, of course."

"You're sure, Louisa?" Her eyes are tired. She looks into her hands. I guess what future she can see in them is not a happy one. She does not look well. Can she be sick?

"I'm quite sure, Mrs. Ropes."

I go out in the yard, where an ambulance is waiting. Surgeon McClintock rushes out the back door, putting on his coat. In his haste, he doesn't notice that he has dropped his scarf. I pick it up, shake off the snow, and get into the ambulance beside him.

"Thank you, Nurse. We're full up with sick men, and I'm put out that I must drop everything to see to some colored shirker."

"You don't know he's shamming until you've seen him," I reply tartly.

Affronted, he withdraws into the tent of his self-esteem to sulk.

At the foot of Jefferson Street, the ambulance rattles on board the ferry. The stolid horses neither shy nor fret as it lurches toward Mason's Island. The heavy boat breaks the thin ice, which gathers on its blunt bow like a white moss. A dirty stalk of smoke rises above a sheet-metal stack. Up above, the arches of the Aqueduct Bridge jump in nervous arcs across the water. Behind me loom the Georgetown hills, winter trees bare as spokes. I can make out the college, the porch of a former slave owner's house, and—three miles to the east—the Capitol's white cast-iron dome. The ambulance rumbles onto shore. The driver exchanges a few remarks with the ferryman before clicking his tongue and fanning the horses. On its iron-shod wheels, the ambulance lumbers over a corduroy road through a stand of fir trees leading to Camp Greene.

Don't you find it strange, Louisa, that you should come to this place in the river twice in the same day? Is it Fate, which has replaced Divine Providence in the minds of those who have broken with God but cannot disenthrall themselves of the idea of a ruling destiny? Is it the hand of Fate that has dealt unlucky cards to the maimed and the dying, or is it the luck of the draw that has wrecked them?

Brisk up, Louisa! You follow that particular line of inquiry at your peril.

Even under the exhausted sky, the white tents are striking, as is the company of black soldiers drilling on the parade ground "in full sight and under the very noses of the secessionists of Georgetown," the white officer in charge of the negroes is pleased to say as the surgeon and I walk toward the makeshift hospital. The ambulance goes on to the stable, where the driver can see to the horses. I feel all swimmy-headed. I wish I could lie down in the straw.

"There's your patient," says the officer, who has stopped to feed the stove. "I'm Captain Bragg. Not that it matters." He smiles inscrutably and breaks a stick of firewood over his knee.

"McClintock," says the surgeon gruffly, introducing himself.

I don't bother to give my name, and the captain doesn't ask it.

We approach a cot not as two priests would the blood and body of Christ laid out on an altar but as butchers do a carcass on the block. A man, who is likely younger than the forty-some years written on his face, lies on his back. I keep myself from flinching at the nauseous odor. When McClintock removes the blanket, the gangrenous foot, ankle, and shin do not surprise me. The patient groans. The Earth made such an anguished cry, I think, when Cain slew his brother. It will make it one last time when it flies from its axle. Louisa, a man's groan is piteous enough without your being fanciful!

Holding a stick of wood, Bragg looks as if he might beat the surgeon's brains out with it for having caused the wounded man pain. The white captain has charge over him and is bound to consider his well-being, regardless of the color of his skin. His momentary ire spent, he tosses the stick into the belly of the stove. He follows us outside to spare the negro.

"We'll have to amputate," says McClintock brusquely.

"The foot," says Bragg, scratching his jaw.

"More than that."

They could be two carpenters discussing a length of board.

"He cauterized it with gunpowder," says Bragg in a voice mixed with awe and perplexity at the lengths humans will go to achieve their ends. "You could've heard his scream in Richmond. Will you take him across to Union Hospital?"

"I don't think he can stand the jostling. I'll do the best I can for him here."

"I'll scare up a couple of boys to help. Want some whiskey, Major?"

"For myself, yes," replies McClintock. "I've brought chloroform for the negro."

Bragg goes into one of the barracks and shortly returns, carrying a bottle. He is accompanied by two colored soldiers, who set a laundry tub of water on the stove.

"Thank you kindly," says McClintock, having drunk off the neck.

"Nothing beats Kentucky whiskey," says Bragg, smacking his lips. "It's getting scarce as hen's teeth—damn this war!"

"Hold him down," McClintock says bluntly when the water on the stove has come to a boil.

We do as we're told. I intend to bear witness, but feeling the blood drain from my face, I turn away.

The surgeon quickly saws the man's leg several inches below the knee. I pick it up and wrap it in a blanket, as if he has delivered a baby instead of a rotted limb. (Have you gone crazy, Louisa? I think you have, poor dear.) The soldiers regard me nervously. The surgeon ties off the arteries with silk thread, scrapes the end and edges of the bone, pulls the flap of skin across the wound, and sews it closed. Leaving a hole to drain the stump, he covers it with an isinglass plaster.

"Let him rest before we take him back," says McClintock, wiping the saw blade on his gory apron.

"Doctor, I've some blackberry brandy in my quarters."

"Much obliged. Nurse, keep an eye on him." He points his saw at the unconscious negro. "Yell if anything seems amiss."

"Yes, sir." Piqued by the Imp of the Perverse, I almost ask if he thinks the man is malingering.

The two officers walk off, leaving me with the patient and two black soldiers. I catch them glancing sidelong at me. I suppose they think I'm another crazy white woman. I begin to croon over the swaddled leg. I stare at them, as a lunatic would, enjoying their uneasiness.

"If you don't need us, ma'am, we'll be getting back," says one of the pair.

"I put an antic disposition on," as the Danish prince said; I stick out my tongue at them and laugh. Take care, Louisa, that they don't stick you in the asylum.

The two soldiers beat a hasty retreat.

McClintock returns, flush with spirits. I glance at the negro's bandaged stump and, for an instant, believe that the surgeon has cut off the wrong leg—a misfortune that has happened when the sawbones is soused. "Let's head back, Miss Alcott."

The ambulance is waiting. The horses are sick. McClintock and the driver lift the stretcher. The canvas sags under the weight of the unconscious negro (unless he is dead). They put him in beside me. The ambulance jolts as the horses assume their load. (Most certainly the man is dead!) We roll toward the ferry landing. I wave to Lucy Higgs, who is carrying a wicker basket of washed and folded sheets. Her face is radiant. I watch her vanish behind a screen of jack pines. I smile at the cunning with which I have concealed the swaddled leg inside my cape.

As we cross the river to Georgetown, I resist the temptation to look at the place where the rocky shoal and the scrub oak are. If there is a body snagged in its branches, I don't want to know of it. My head hurts. My eyes pain me; I close them as the ambulance rocks on its springs.

"Mr. Whitman. I'm Bronson Alcott's daughter Louisa."

"Miss Alcott. I've seen you at the Union and Armory Square hospitals, without realizing that you're Amos Bronson's girl."

"We are both, it seems, caring for the casualties of this awful war."

"It breaks the heart to see the dear boys suffer!"

"I didn't think much of you, at first."

"Your frankness is refreshing, Miss Alcott. I hate dissemblers and frauds."

"As do I, though I fear I sometimes am one."

"You look tired, Louisa."

"I am—right down in my bones. I could stretch out beside this negro and shut my eyes for an eternity."

"I've heard your friend Mr. Emerson say that eternity is a mighty long stretch of time."

"Matron says I must rest."

"Then you should."

McClintock is folding and unfolding his hands. I refuse to speculate on the meaning of his gesture. My mind's worn-out. Let meaning seep into the ground like horses' stale. Let the taut cable relax that connects the intellect with the body and composes the fateful being that bears the quite arbitrary name of Louisa May Alcott.

No, I won't relax! I must look at the bundle of rags. I must search the dead house for Henry and John Sulie.

"Be still, Louisa," says Whitman kindly. He crowds my attic room. "You're burning with fever. Mrs. Ropes is also down with it. . . . No, you can't get up! You must stay in bed. You're very sick, my dear."

I've a sharp pain in my side; my head aches; the room turns giddily on its axis. If this keeps up much longer, Earth will unravel like a ball of wool.

"Take this, Louisa."

"What is it?"

"Calomel. It'll keep your bowels and pores open."

He gives me the blue pill to swallow. I taste licorice and rose water. My mouth and gums burn. He closes my eyes with his big hand.

"Lie still, dear girl," he croons.

"Poor thing," murmurs Lucy Higgs.

"God, heal this child!" says Preacher John, as though he's dunning Him.

"Will she live?" asks Fanny, wearing roses on her chest.

Rooting in my mouth with a blistered tongue, I feel the rough place where the dentist filled a tooth on the day I left Boston. There hasn't been enough time since my arrival in Washington for it to have worn smooth.

I wonder if I am to die here.

. . . *the Piper advanced and the children followed,*
And when all were in to the very last,
The door in the mountain-side shut fast.

ENTRIES FROM MY JOURNAL

Made in Concord
When I Was Well Again

February. — Recovered my senses after three weeks of delirium, and was told I had had a very bad typhoid fever, had nearly died, and was still very sick. All of which seemed rather curious, for I remembered nothing of it. Found a queer, thin, big-eyed face when I looked in the glass; didn't know myself at all; and when I tried to walk discovered that I couldn't, and cried because my legs wouldn't go.

I remember having thought with absolute conviction that I had married a stout, handsome Spaniard, dressed in black velvet, with very soft hands, and a voice that was continually saying, "Lie still, my dear!" This was Mother, I suspect; but with all the comfort I often found in her presence, there was blended an awful fear of the Spanish spouse who was always coming after me, appearing out of closets, in at windows, or threatening me dreadfully all night long. I appealed to the Pope, and really got up and made a touching plea in something meant for Latin, they tell me. Once I went to heaven, and found it a twi-light place, with people darting through the air in a queer way,—all very busy, and dismal, and ordinary. I wished I hadn't come.

Postscript. Received $10 for my labors in Washing-ton. Had all my hair, a yard and a half long, cut off, and went into caps like a grandma. Felt badly about losing my one beauty. Never mind, it might have been my head, and a wig outside is better than a loss of wits inside.

WALT WHITMAN

Washington City
JANUARY 21, 1863

"Mr. Whitman."

"Miss Dix." I tip my hat to her, determined to be cordial.

"I believe you know Mr. Alcott, of Concord."

"We're acquaintances," I reply, puzzled. The Dragon seldom speaks to me, and I haven't seen Bronson since we had a drink together at Taylor's saloon on Broadway. He called me "the very God Pan—as hard to tame as Thoreau." I was delighted.

"Then you must know his daughter Louisa."

"Of her; I've never met the lady."

"She's been a nurse at Union Hospital since December."

"I didn't know. When I've time, I'll stop and pay her my respects."

"That is why I asked to see you. Miss Alcott is in a bad way. Her father's come to take her home. They've been staying at Willard's until she can travel."

"I'm sorry to hear it. I'll go straight away."

"Please give Louisa our love. Mr. Whitman, I wonder if you'd further oblige me by taking her a gift." She goes into her office and returns with a basket containing barley wine, tea, medicine, cologne, a fan, a pillow, and a Bible. "Say that it's from all of us. We've grown fond of Miss Alcott and are very sorry she's ill."

"I'll be glad to."

"Tell her she's in our prayers." Miss Dix lowers her voice. "I don't know if you've heard, but Matron Ropes has just died of the same illness."

Feeling oafish, I take off my hat. "I didn't know. She was a good soul."

"She was indeed. Good afternoon, Mr. Whitman, and thank you." She pauses and then says, "And thank you for your kindness to the boys."

I leave, feeling blessed, like a nun who has just swallowed the Host.

I cross the frozen canal and the lifeless grounds outside the President's House. I hurry to the Willard Hotel, only to be told that the Alcotts left for Boston this morning. I hasten to the Baltimore and Ohio depot, but the train has gone. I stand beside the empty tracks, holding the basket of cheer, which seems to me now the decoration for a grave.

I think that all the grass has been dug up for graves and will not grow again, that winter is the only season, and that I have striven for nothing, written nothing of any use, and have been nothing but a fraud.

I imagine myself kneeling beside the track and pressing an ear against it as I did long ago in Brooklyn to hear the distant thunder of a train. How strange that subterranean sound made me feel, as though I were listening to the disgruntled Earth or the Minotaur anguished and desperate in its loneliness.

I look up the tracks toward the North, where farmhouses, shops, factories, and schools are being emptied of young men and where—in parlors at Concord and Boston—Transcendentalists worry the ancient bone of God. I would rather sit in Pfaff's beer cellar, winding my arms about my comrades, than squat like a toad at the feet of the Almighty. There is nothing to do, except to pretend that doing matters. There is no word that will be of comfort, no revelation for a mind that has become like a king post slipped from the crossbeam or an anchor from the anchor chain—no saving grace in a heart that is dead. There is nothing for our mouths, except to eat and drink and kiss another's lips and make believe it is enough.

Aqueduct Bridge and Mason's Island on the Potomac River. (Library of Congress)

AFTERWORD

Afar down I see the huge first Nothing

—Walt Whitman

I HAVE WRITTEN A NOVEL and invented much, but the broad outline of the story is factual. Walt Whitman and Louisa May Alcott were living and working in Washington in January 1863, he as a deputy for the Christian Commission and she as a nurse at Union Hospital, a mile and a half from Armory Square Hospital, where his volunteer work as a sanctioned visitor and de facto wound dresser was centered. Although they never met, it is not unimaginable that they could have seen each other, as the novel has it.

At the time, Whitman was a part-time copyist in the army paymaster's office and did go to Mason's Island to pay the U.S. Colored Troops. Pete Doyle was a horsecar conductor on the Washington and Georgetown Railroad, and Whitman often kept him company at night on the route—not in 1863, but after the war, when the two become friends and, arguably, lovers. Whitman's relationship with the O'Connors was more or less as I sketched it. Mathew

Brady did have a studio on the fourth floor of a brick building with cast-iron colonettes at 625 Pennsylvania Avenue during the war. Brady did take the poet's likeness in his Daguerrean Miniature Gallery on Broadway before the war. All that I have written about Whitman's first month in Washington is credible. I have, however, crowded the month with incidents that likely would have occurred less compactly. Alcott's brief stay in the capital city established the duration of the novel.

To discover that Whitman's view of black slaves and freedmen was unenlightened (a timid word) is disheartening. His ambition to rhapsodize comprehensively led him to write, "I am the poet of slaves and of the masters of slaves / I am the poet of the body / I am." The racist opinions to which he gives utterance in this novel are in his own words. "In comparison with this slaughter, I don't care for the niggers" is reported by Justin Kaplan in his *Walt Whitman: A Life*. ("No! no! I should not like to see the nigger in the saddle—it seems unnatural" appears in Roy Morris's *The Better Angel*. I struck it from the final draft of this novel—afraid that the weight of Whitman's prejudice would likely obscure, for the modern reader, the complicated personality of a man whose published work was an assault on the many prejudices of his time.)

When our heroes—and Whitman the writer is one of mine—behave badly, we like to say that they were a product of the times. I fear it is a weak defense.

And yet Whitman the man did an immense service to the casualties in a war that killed and maimed upward of 650,000. He made some six hundred visits and ministered to tens of thousands of wounded soldiers—both Union and Confederate (as if he himself intended to "bind up the nation's wounds")—during his four years at the capital's hospitals. (Whitman estimated "from eighty thousand to a hundred thousand of the wounded and sick.") He was a volunteer in the wards and drew from a paltry salary earned in several clerical capacities to pay for the many treats he never failed to bring his "boys." And of course, Whitman the man bequeathed to us one of our literature's landmarks. As inadequate an apology as all this is, I find I must leave it at that.

Louisa May Alcott's youthful infatuation with Thoreau and, more especially, Emerson, of whom she said "he is the god of my idolatry, and has been for years" is factual; so, too, was the intensity of her brief investment of feeling in John Suhre, or Sulie, as she has it in her journals. Her entry at the end of the novel, in which she vividly describes her febrile delusions, is from her journal, as is her record of her sister Lizzie's death. Alcott's harping on money was indeed the case: "I'm resolved to take Fate by the throat and shake a living out of her." So, too, was her continual chafing against the restraints imposed on her sex: "I long to be a man, but as I can't fight, I will content myself working for those who can."

Lincoln did visit the capital's hospitals, black churches, and the Naval Observatory to take comfort in the stars. Matron Hannah Ropes and Superintendent Dorothea Dix were, largely, as I have presented them, though vastly simplified. Miss Dix may have been known as "Dragon Dix" for her sternness, but her responsibilities as superintendent of nurses for the Union army were enormous. During her career, she was a frequent petitioner of Congress on behalf of U.S. prison reform and the treatment of the nation's indigent mentally ill. Hannah Ropes did bring charges of corruption and abuse against Union Hospital's chief surgeon and its steward to Secretary of War Stanton. Also true is Nurse Hawley's objection to Walt Whitman's dubious character, expressed in a letter to her brigadier general husband. Whitman admired the compassionate, efficient nurse Harriet Wright, though I have imagined his flirtatiousness and their having lunch together.

Ralph Waldo Emerson, called "Waldo" by his friends (his wife preferred to address him as "Mr. Emerson"), did indeed write: "What argument, what evidence can avail against the power of that one word *niggers*? The man of the world annihilates the whole combined force of all the antislavery societies of the world by pronouncing it." He is worthy—in this intolerant age of ours—of our respect. Readers of the previous books in the American Novels series *The Port-Wine Stain, The Wreckage of Eden,* and *Feast Day of the Cannibals* will recall having met Edward Fenzil, army surgeon, and Robert Winter, army chaplain. I took the liberty of substituting my fictitious Fenzil for the actual Dr. John Winslow, a surgeon at Union Hospital, who was enamored of Louisa and spent time in her company. It was with Robert Browning's poetry and not Edgar Poe's prose that Winslow did his best to woo Miss Alcott, who remained Miss Alcott until her death in 1888. She spent the years following her removal from Washington subject to illnesses that we now know to be the result of mercury poisoning. Calomel (the "blue pill"), with which she was dosed, contains that element.

Among the novel's omissions necessary to dramatic pace and tension is the pneumonia that Alcott contracted at the beginning of January, along with Matron Ropes, who died of it. Alcott's constitution was weakened even before she was sickened by typhoid.

I took pains to get the geography and city plan right; for the latter, I referred often to the 1862 Johnson & Ward map of Washington and Georgetown. Yes, the novel is a work of fiction and carries the usual disclaimers. But I have come to respect the lives of my historical characters as they were lived in actuality and strive to be as factual as a novel's dramatic effect permits. (My striving for fidelity to the past—in this novel and the preceding ones in the series—has been assisted by Bellevue Literary Press's copyeditor, Carol Edwards.) On occasion, I allow my historical subjects to utter their own recorded words—slightly altered or rearranged, if grammar or sense dictates. I borrowed liberally from Whitman's poetry and prose, as well as from others' recollections of him. (I may be forgiven any anachronistic quotations, if Whitman students or scholars will consider them as thoughts in the poet's head or journals, preceding their official publication.) Matron Ropes's speech beginning "I have no office to lose or gain" is, mostly, in her own words, as recorded in her diary. Preacher Holmes's homily is based on "De Sun Do Move," a sermon delivered by the fiery black Baptist preacher John Jasper, of Virginia, who, incidentally, preached to Confederate soldiers during the war. (To have indicated my borrowings with single quotation marks inside invented utterances set off by double quotation marks would be confusing and ungainly. Asterisks or superscripts would be more intrusive.)

I attempted to imitate the voices of Whitman and Alcott. Readers unfamiliar with her journals and especially *Hospital Sketches* may be surprised by the impudent wit and humor. Remarkably modern in tone and feeling, *Hospital Sketches* made Alcott's reputation as a serious author. Its contents are frank and its manner breezy, brash, and Dickensian. As she described the book: "to the serious-minded party who objected to a tone of levity in some portions of the Sketches, I can only say that it is a part of my religion to look well after the cheerfulness of life . . ." My emulation of Whitman's style was aided by an immersion in his poetry and in his prose work *Specimen Days.* Although he considered himself a populist and a poet of democracy, his writing is more formal than Alcott's, as one might expect of an author addressing posterity.

That these two influential recorders of life in wartime Washington City did, in fact, circulate between Union Hospital and Armory Square Hospital in January 1863 enabled me to present two distinct views on one of the most consequential periods in the nation's history.

Postscript: January 13, 2021. As I am finishing the fifth draft of this novel, the House of Representatives is debating an article of impeachment charging President Trump with sedition, following the invasion of the Capitol last week by many thousands of violent insurrectionists. In advance of Joe Biden's inauguration as America's next president, our capital city prepares for another possible uprising. Not since the time in which this novel is set has Washington resembled an armed camp.

ACKNOWLEDGMENTS

For insight into the lives and works of Whitman and Alcott, as well as into wartime Washington, I relied on the following sources: *The Better Angel: Walt Whitman in the Civil War*, by Roy Morris, Jr; *Civil War Nurse: The Diary and Letters of Hannah Ropes*; *Hospital Sketches*, by Louisa May Alcott, edited by Alice Fahs; *John Jasper: The Unmatched Negro Philosopher and Preacher*, by William Eldridge Hatcher; the Library of Congress for primary sources such as maps, newspapers, and songs; *Louisa May Alcott: Her Life, Letters, and Journals*, edited by Ednah Dow Cheney; *Louisa May Alcott: A Personal Biography*, by Susan Cheever; *Memoranda During the War*, by Walt Whitman; The Walt Whitman Archive (an online resource); *Walt Whitman: A Life*, by Justin Kaplan; *Walt Whitman Speaks*, edited by Brenda Wineapple; *Whitman: Poetry and Prose*, published by the Library of America; and *Women at the Front: Hospital Workers in Civil War America*, by Jane E. Schultz.

Holy Sh*t: A Brief History of Swearing, by Melissa Mohr, is a gift to writers of historical fiction who wish to add salt to their stew.

I thank the Copyright and Permissions Department of Harvard University Press for pointing out that the Emily Dickinson poem "To fill a Gap" (J 546/F 647) is in the public domain. I return the courtesy by citing its source.*

The 1863 photograph of Whitman is published online at The Walt Whitman Archive and is in the public domain. The source of the digital image is the Clifton Waller Barrett Library of American Literature, Albert and Shirley Small Special Collections Library, University of Virginia.

For ten years, I have had the privilege and joy of an association with Bellevue Literary Press. The press is what every writer of literary fiction hopes to find but may never do so. My gratitude to Erika Goldman, publisher and editorial director; Jerome Lowenstein, M.D., founding publisher; Laura Hart, publishing assistant; Molly Mikolowski, publicist; Joe Gannon, production and design consultant; Carol Edwards, copyeditor; and Elana Rosenthal, proofreader, is boundless.

---

* *The Poems of Emily Dickinson,* ed. Thomas H. Johnson (Cambridge: Belknap Press of Harvard University Press, copyright © 1951, 1955, 1979, 1983 by the President and Fellows of Harvard College).

THE LAST WORD
BELONGS TO WHITMAN

WALT WHITMAN,
AS PHOTOGRAPHED BY ALEXANDER GARDNER,
IN WASHINGTON, 1863
(THE WALT WHITMAN ARCHIVE)

*Literature is big only in one way—when used as an
aid in the growth of the humanities—a furthering of
the cause of the masses—a means whereby men may be
revealed to each other as brothers.*

BELLEVUE LITERARY PRESS is devoted to publishing
literary fiction and nonfiction at the intersection of
the arts and sciences because we believe that science and
the humanities are natural companions for understanding
the human experience. We feature exceptional literature
that explores the nature of consciousness, embodiment,
and the underpinnings of the social contract. With
each book we publish, our goal is to foster a rich,
interdisciplinary dialogue that will forge new tools for
thinking and engaging with the world.

To support our press and its mission, and for our full
catalogue of published titles, please visit us at blpress.org.

BELLEVUE LITERARY PRESS
New York